melville house classics

THE ART OF THE NOVELLA

CARMEN

CARMEN

PROSPER MÉRIMÉE

TRANSLATED BY GEORGE BURNHAM IVES

MELVILLE HOUSE
BROOKLYN • LONDON

CARMEN BY PROSPER MÉRIMÉE

ORIGINALLY PUBLISHED IN 1903 BY G. P. PUTNAM'S SONS

FIRST MELVILLE HOUSE PRINTING: AUGUST 2013

MELVILLE HOUSE PUBLISHING
145 PLYMOUTH STREET
BROOKLYN, NY 11201

AND

8 BLACKSTOCK MEWS
ISLINGTON
LONDON N4 2BT

MHPBOOKS.COM FACEBOOK.COM/MHPBOOKS @MELVILLEHOUSE

LIBRARY OF CONGRESS CONTROL NUMBER: 2013943159

ISBN: 978-1-61219-226-0

BOOK DESIGN: CHRISTOPHER KING, BASED ON
A SERIES DESIGN BY DAVID KONOPKA

PRINTED IN THE UNITED STATES OF AMERICA
1 3 5 7 9 10 8 6 4 2

Πᾶσα γυνὴ χόλος ἐστίν· ἔχει δ᾽ἀγαθὰς δύο ὥρας
Τὴν μίαν ἐν θαλάμῳ, τὴν μίαν ἐν θανάτῳ.

PALLADAS

CARMEN

I

I had always suspected the geographers of not knowing what they were talking about when they placed the battle-field of Munda in the country of the Bastuli-Poeni, near the modern Monda, some two leagues north of Marbella. According to my own conjectures concerning the text of the anonymous author of the *Bellum Hispaniense*, and in view of certain information collected in the Duke of Ossuna's excellent library, I believed that we should seek in the vicinity of Montilla the memorable spot where for the last time Caesar played double or quits against the champions of the republic. Happening to be in Andalusia in the early autumn of 1830, I made quite a long excursion for the purpose of setting at rest such doubts as I still entertained. A memoir which I propose to publish ere long will, I trust, leave no further uncertainty in the minds of all honest archaeologists. Pending the time when my deliverance shall solve at last the geographical problem which is now holding all the learning of Europe in suspense, I propose to tell you a little story; it has no bearing on the question of the actual location of Munda.

I had hired a guide and two horses at Cordova, and had taken the field with no other impedimenta than Caesar's *Commentaries* and a shirt or two. On a certain day, as I wandered over the more elevated portion of the plain of Cachena, worn out with fatigue, dying with thirst, and scorched by a sun of molten lead, I was wishing with all my heart that Caesar and Pompey's sons were in the devil's grip, when I spied, at a considerable distance from the path I was following, a tiny greensward, studded with reeds and rushes, which indicated the proximity of a spring. In fact, as I drew nearer, I found that what had seemed to be a greensward was a marshy tract through which a stream meandered, issuing apparently from a narrow ravine between two high buttresses of the Sierra de Cabra. I concluded that by ascending the stream I should find cooler water, fewer leeches and frogs, and perhaps a bit of shade among the cliffs. As we rode into the gorge my horse whinnied, and another horse, which I could not see, instantly answered. I had ridden barely a hundred yards when the gorge, widening abruptly, disclosed a sort of natural amphitheatre, entirely shaded by the high cliffs which surrounded it. It was impossible to find a spot which promised the traveller a more attractive sojourn. At the foot of perpendicular cliffs, the spring came bubbling forth and fell into a tiny basin carpeted with sand as white as snow. Five or six fine live-oaks, always sheltered from the wind and watered by the spring, grew upon its brink and covered it with their dense shade; and all about the basin, a fine, sheeny grass promised a softer bed than one could find at any inn within a radius of ten leagues.

The honour of discovering so attractive a spot did not belong to me. A man was already reposing there, and was asleep in all probability when I rode in. Roused by the neighing of the horses, he had risen, and had walked towards his horse, which had taken advantage of his master's slumber to make a hearty meal on the grass in the immediate neighbourhood. He was a young fellow, of medium height, but of robust aspect, and with a proud and distrustful expression. His complexion, which might once have been fine, had become darker than his hair through the action of the sun. He held his horse's halter in one hand and in the other a blunderbuss with a copper barrel. I will admit that at first blush the blunderbuss and the forbidding air of its bearer took me a little by surprise; but I had ceased to believe in robbers, because I had heard so much said about them and had never met one. Moreover, I had seen so many honest farmers going to market armed to the teeth that the sight of a firearm did not justify me in suspecting the stranger's moral character.—"And then, too," I said to myself, "what would he do with my shirts and my Elzevir Caesar?" So I saluted the man with the blunderbuss with a familiar nod, and asked him smilingly if I had disturbed his sleep.

He eyed me from head to foot without replying; then, as if satisfied by his examination, he scrutinised no less closely my guide, who rode up at that moment. I saw that the latter turned pale and stopped in evident alarm. "An unfortunate meeting!" I said to myself. But prudence instantly counselled me to betray no uneasiness. I dismounted, told the guide to remove the horses' bridles, and, kneeling by the spring, I plunged my face and hands in the water; then I took a long draught and lay flat on my stomach, like the wicked soldiers of Gideon.

But I kept my eyes on my guide and the stranger. The former drew near, sorely against his will; the other seemed to have no evil designs upon us, for he had set his horse at liberty once more, and his blunderbuss, which he had held at first in a horizontal position, was now pointed towards the ground.

As it seemed to me inexpedient to take umbrage at the small amount of respect shown to my person, I stretched myself out on the grass, and asked the man with the blunderbuss, in a careless tone, if he happened to have a flint and steel about him. At the same time I produced my cigar-case. The stranger, still without a word, felt in his pocket, took out his flint and steel and courteously struck a light for me. Evidently he was becoming tamer, for he sat down opposite me, but did not lay aside his weapon. When my cigar was lighted; I selected the best of those that remained and asked him if he smoked.

"Yes, señor," he replied.

Those were the first words that he had uttered, and I noticed that he did not pronounce the *s* after the Andalusian fashion,* whence I concluded that he was a traveller like myself, minus the archaeologist.

* The Andalusians aspirate the *s*, and in pronunciation confound it with *c* soft and *z*, which the Spaniards pronounce like the English *th*. It is possible to recognize an Andalusian by the one word *señor*.

"You will find this rather good," I said, offering him a genuine Havana regalia.

He bent his head slightly, lighted his cigar by mine, thanked me with another nod, then began to smoke with every appearance of very great enjoyment.

"Ah!" he exclaimed, as he discharged the first puff slowly through his mouth and his nostrils. "How long it is since I have had a smoke!"

In Spain, a cigar offered and accepted establishes hospitable relations, just as the sharing of bread and salt does in the East. My man became more talkative than I had hoped. But, although he claimed to live in the *partido* of Montilla, he seemed to be but ill-acquainted with the country. He did not know the name of the lovely valley where we were; he could not mention any village in the neighbourhood; and, lastly, when I asked him whether he had seen any ruined walls thereabouts, or any tiles with raised edges, or any carved stones, he admitted that he had never paid any attention to such things. By way of compensation he exhibited much expert knowledge of horses. He criticised mine, which was not very difficult; then he gave me the genealogy of his, which came from the famous stud of Cordova; a noble animal in very truth, and so proof against fatigue, according to his master, that he had once travelled thirty leagues in a day, at a gallop or a fast trot. In the middle of his harangue the stranger paused abruptly, as if he were surprised and angry with himself for having said too much.

"You see, I was in a hurry to get to Cordova," he added,

with some embarrassment. "I had to present a petition to the judges in the matter of a lawsuit."

As he spoke, he glanced at my guide, Antonio, who lowered his eyes.

The cool shade and the spring were so delightful to me that I remembered some slices of excellent ham which my friends at Montilla had put in my guide's wallet. I bade him produce them, and I invited the stranger to join me in my impromptu collation. If he had not smoked for a long while, it seemed probable to me that he had not eaten for at least forty-eight hours. He devoured the food like a starved wolf. It occurred to me that our meeting was a providential affair for the poor fellow. My guide meanwhile ate little, drank still less, and did not talk at all, although from the very beginning of our journey he had revealed himself to me in the guise of an unparalleled chatterbox. Our guest's presence seemed to embarrass him, and a certain distrust kept them at arm's length from each other, but I was unable to divine its cause.

The last crumbs of the bread and ham had vanished; each of us had smoked a second cigar; I ordered the guide to put the bridles on our horses, and I was about to take leave of my new friend, when he asked me where I intended to pass the night.

I replied, before I had noticed a signal from my guide, that I was going on to the Venta del Cuervo.

"A wretched place for a man like you, señor. I am going there, and if you will allow me to accompany you, we will ride together."

"With great pleasure," I replied, mounting my horse.

My guide, who was holding my stirrup, made another signal with his eyes. I answered it with a shrug of my shoulders, as if to assure him that I was perfectly unconcerned, and we set forth.

Antonio's mysterious signs, his evident uneasiness, a few words that had escaped from the stranger, and, above all, his gallop of thirty leagues, and the far from plausible explanation of it which he had offered, had already formed my opinion concerning our travelling companion. I had no doubt that I had fallen in with a smuggler, perhaps a highwayman; but what did it matter to me? I was sufficiently acquainted with the Spanish character to be very sure that I had nothing to fear from a man who had broken bread and smoked with me. His very presence was a certain protection against any unpleasant meetings. Furthermore, I was very glad to know what manner of man a brigand is. One does not see them every day, and there is a certain charm in finding oneself in the company of a dangerous individual, especially when one finds him to be gentle and tame.

I hoped to lead the stranger by degrees to the point of making me his confidant, and despite my guide's meaning winks, I turned the conversation to the subject of highway robbers. Be it understood that I spoke of them with great respect. There was in Andalusia at that time a celebrated brigand named José Maria, whose exploits were on every tongue.

"Suppose I were riding beside José Maria!" I said to myself.

I told such stories as I knew concerning that hero—all to

his credit, by the way,—and I expressed in warm terms my admiration for his gallantry and his generosity.

"José Maria is a villain pure and simple," observed the stranger, coldly.

"Is he doing himself justice?" I thought. "Or is this merely an excess of modesty on his part?" For, by dint of observing my companion closely, I had succeeded in applying to him the description of José Maria which I had seen placarded on the gates of many a town in Andalusia. "Yes, it is certainly he: fair hair, blue eyes, large mouth, fine teeth, small hands; a shirt of fine linen, velvet jacket with silver buttons, white leather gaiters, a bay horse. There is no doubt of it! But I will respect his incognito."

We arrived at the *venta*. It was the sort of place that he had described, that is to say, one of the vilest taverns that I had seen as yet. A large room served as kitchen, dining-room, and bedroom. The fire was kindled on a flat stone in the middle of the room, and the smoke emerged through a hole in the roof, or rather hung about it, forming a dense cloud a few feet from the floor. Stretched on the ground along the walls could be seen some five or six worn mule-blankets; they were the beds of the guests. Some twenty yards from the house, or rather from the single room which I have described, was a sort of shed, which did duty as a stable. In this attractive abode there were no other human beings, for the moment at least, than an old woman and a little girl of eight or ten years, both as black as soot and clad in shocking rags.

"Behold," I said to myself, "all that remains of the population of the ancient Munda Boetica! O Caesar! O Sextus

Pompey! how surprised you would be, should you return to earth!"

At sight of my companion, the old woman uttered an exclamation of surprise.

"Ah! Señor Don José!" she cried.

Don José frowned and raised his hand with an authoritative gesture which instantly silenced the old woman. I turned to my guide, and with an imperceptible sign gave him to understand that there was nothing that he could tell me concerning the man with whom I was about to pass the night.

The supper was better than I anticipated. On a small table about a foot high we were served with an aged rooster, fricasseed with rice and an abundance of peppers; then with peppers in oil; and lastly with *gaspacho*, a sort of pepper salad. Three dishes thus highly seasoned compelled us to have frequent recourse to a skin of Montilla wine, which was delicious. After we had eaten, happening to spy a mandolin hanging on the wall,—there are mandolins everywhere in Spain,—I asked the little girl who waited on us if she knew how to play it.

"No," she replied, "but Don José plays it so well!"

"Be good enough," I said to him, "to sing me something; I am passionately fond of your national music."

"I can refuse no request of such a gallant gentleman, who gives me such excellent cigars," said Don José, good-naturedly.

And, having asked for the mandolin, he sang to his own accompaniment. His voice was rough, but very agreeable, the tune melancholy and weird; as for the words, I did not understand a syllable.

"If I am not mistaken," I said, "that is not a Spanish air. It resembles the *zorzicos* which I have heard in the Provinces,* and the words must be Basque."

"Yes," replied Don José, with a gloomy air.

He placed the mandolin on the floor, and sat with folded arms, gazing at the dying fire with a strange expression of melancholy. His face at once noble and fierce, lighted by a lamp that stood on the low table, reminded me of Milton's Satan. Perhaps, like him, my companion was thinking of the sojourn that he had left, of the banishment that he had incurred by a sin. I tried to revive the conversation, but he did not answer, absorbed as he was in his sad thoughts. The old woman had already retired in one corner of the room, behind an old torn blanket suspended by a cord. The little girl had followed her to that retreat, reserved for the fair sex. Thereupon my guide rose and invited me to accompany him to the stable; but at that suggestion Don José, as if suddenly awakened, asked him roughly where he was going.

"To the stable," was the guide's reply.

"What for? The horses have their feed. Sleep here; the señor will not object."

"I am afraid the señor's horse is sick; I would like the señor to see him; perhaps he will know what to do for him."

It was evident that Antonio wished to speak to me in private; but I had no desire to arouse Don José's suspicions, and,

* That is, the *privileged provinces*, which enjoy special *fueros*, namely, Alava, Biscay, Guipuzcoa, and a part of Navarre. Basque is the language spoken in those provinces.

in view of the footing on which we then stood, it seemed to me that the wisest course was to show the most entire confidence. So I told Antonio that I understood nothing about horses, and that I wished to sleep. Don José went with him to the stable, whence he soon returned alone. He told me that nothing was the matter with the horse, but that my guide considered him such a valuable beast that he was rubbing him with his jacket to make him sweat, and that he proposed to pass the night in that delectable occupation. Meanwhile I had stretched myself out on the mule-blankets, carefully wrapped in my cloak, in order not to come in contact with them. After apologising for the liberty he took in taking his place beside me, Don José lay down before the door, not without renewing the priming of his blunderbuss, which he took care to place under the wallet which served him for a pillow. Five minutes after we had bade each other good-night we were both sound asleep.

I had believed that I was tired enough to be able to sleep even on such a couch; but after about an hour, a very unpleasant itching roused me from my first nap. As soon as I realised the nature of it, I rose, convinced that it would be better to pass the night in the open air than beneath that inhospitable roof. I walked to the door on tiptoe, stepped over Don José, who was sleeping the sleep of the just, and exerted such care that I left the houses without waking him. Near the door was a broad wooden bench; I lay down upon it, and bestowed myself as comfortably as possible to finish the night. I was just closing my eyes for the second time, when it seemed to me that I saw the shadows of a man and a horse pass me, both moving without the slightest sound. I sat up, and fancied that I recognised Antonio. Surprised to find him outside of the stable at that time of night, I rose and walked toward him. He had halted, having seen me first.

"Where is he?" he asked in a whisper.

"In the *venta*; he is asleep; he has no fear of fleas. Why are you taking that horse away?"

I noticed then that to avoid making any noise on leaving the shed, Antonio had carefully wrapped the animal's feet in the remnants of an old blanket.

"Speak lower, in God's name!" said Antonio. "Don't you know who that man is? He's José Navarro, the most celebrated bandit in Andalusia. I have been making signs to you all day, but you wouldn't understand."

"Bandit or not, what do I care?" said I. "He has not robbed us, and I'll wager that he has no inclination to do so."

"Very good! but there's a reward of two hundred ducats for whoever causes his capture. I know that there's a detachment of lancers stationed a league and a half from here, and before daybreak I will bring up some stout fellows to take him. I would have taken his horse, but the beast is so vicious that no one but Navarro can go near him."

"The devil take you!" said I. "What harm has the poor fellow done to you that you should denounce him? Besides, are you quite sure that he is the brigand you say he is?"

"Perfectly sure; he followed me to the stable just now and said to me: 'You act as if you knew me; if you tell that honest gentleman who I am, I'll blow your brains out!'—Stay, señor, stay with him; you have nothing to fear. So long as he knows you are here he won't suspect anything."

As we talked we had walked so far from the *venta* that the noise of the horse's shoes could not be heard there. Antonio, in a twinkling, removed the rags in which he had wrapped them, and prepared to mount. I tried to detain him by entreaties and threats.

"I am a poor devil, señor," he said; "two hundred ducats aren't to be thrown away, especially when it's a question of ridding the province of such vermin. But beware! if Navarro wakes, he'll jump for his blunderbuss, and then look out for yourself! I have gone too far to go back; take care of yourself as best you can."

The rascal was already in the saddle; he dug both spurs into the horse, and I soon lost sight of him in the darkness.

I was very angry with my guide, and decidedly uneasy. After a moment's reflection, I decided what to do, and returned to the *venta*. Don José was still asleep, repairing doubtless the effects of the fatigue and vigils of several days of peril. I was obliged to shake him violently in order to rouse him. I shall never forget his fierce glance and the movement that he made to grasp his blunderbuss, which, as a precautionary measure, I had placed at some distance from his couch.

"Señor," I said, "I ask your pardon for waking you; but I have a foolish question to ask you: would you be greatly pleased to see half a dozen lancers ride up to this door?"

He sprang to his feet and demanded in a terrible voice:

"Who told you?"

"It matters little whence the warning comes, provided that it be well founded."

"Your guide has betrayed me, but he shall pay me for it! Where is he?"

"I don't know; in the stable, I think.—But some one told me—"

"Who told you? It couldn't have been the old woman."

"Some one whom I do not know.—But without more words, have you any reason for not awaiting the soldiers, yes or no? If you have, waste no time; if not, good-night, and I ask your pardon for disturbing your sleep."

"Ah! your guide! your guide! I suspected him from the first; but—his account is made up! Farewell, señor! God will repay you for the service you have rendered me. I am not altogether so bad as you think; no, there is still something in me which deserves a gallant man's compassion.—Farewell, señor! I have but one regret, and that is that I cannot pay my debt to you."

"In payment of the service I have rendered you, promise, Don José, to suspect no one, and not to think of revenge. Here, take these cigars, and a pleasant journey to you!"

And I offered him my hand.

He pressed it without replying, took his blunderbuss and his wallet, and after exchanging a few words with the old woman, in an argot which I could not understand, he ran to the shed. A few moments later I heard him galloping across country.

I lay down again on my bench, but I slept no more. I wondered whether I had done right to save a highwayman, perhaps a murderer, from the gibbet, simply because I had eaten ham and rice *à la Valenciennes* with him. Had I not betrayed my guide, who was upholding the cause of the law? Had I not exposed him to the vengeance of a miscreant? But the duties of hospitality!—"The prejudice of a savage!" I said to myself. "I shall be responsible for all the crimes that bandit may commit."—But after all, is it really a prejudice, that instinct of the conscience which is impervious to all argument? Perhaps, in the delicate situation in which I found myself, I could not have taken either course without remorse. I was still in a maze of uncertainty concerning the moral aspect of my action, when I saw half a dozen horsemen approaching, with Antonio, who remained prudently with the rear-guard. I went to meet them and informed them that the brigand had taken flight more than two hours before. The old woman, when questioned by the officer in command, admitted that she knew Navarro, but said that, living alone as she did, she should never have dared to risk her life by denouncing him. She added that it was his custom, whenever he visited her house, to leave in the middle of the night. For my part, I was obliged to go to a place a few leagues away, to show my passport and sign a declaration before an alcalde, after which I was allowed to resume my archaeological investigations. Antonio bore me a grudge, suspecting that it was I who had prevented him from earning the two hundred ducats. However, we parted on friendly terms at Cordova, where I gave him a gratuity as large as the state of my finances would permit.

II

I passed several days at Cordova. I had been told of a certain manuscript in the library of the Dominican convent, in which I was likely to find valuable information concerning the Munda of the ancients. Being very amiably received by the good fathers, I passed the days in their convent, and walked about the city in the evenings. There is always a throng of idlers, about sunset, on the quay that borders the right bank of the Guadalquivir at Cordova. There one inhales the emanations from a tannery which still maintains the ancient celebrity of the district for the manufacture of leather; but, on the other hand, one enjoys a spectacle that has its merits. A few minutes before the Angelus, a great number of women assemble on the river bank, below the quay, which is quite high. No man would dare to join that group. As soon as the Angelus rings, it is supposed to be dark. At the last stroke of the bell, all those women undress and go into the water. Thereupon there is tremendous shouting and laughter and an infernal uproar. From the quay above, the men stare at the bathers, squinting their eyes, but they see very little. However, those vague white shapes outlined against the dark blue of the stream set poetic minds at work; and with a little imagination it is not difficult to conjure up a vision of Diana and her nymphs in the bath, without having to fear the fate of Actaeon. I had been told that on a certain day a number of profane scapegraces clubbed together to grease the palm of the bell-ringer at the cathedral and hire him to ring the Angelus twenty minutes before the legal hour. Although it was still broad daylight, the nymphs of the Guadalquivir did not hesitate, but trusting the Angelus rather than the sun, they fearlessly made their bathing toilet, which is always of the simplest. I was not there. In my day the bell-ringer was incorruptible, the twilight far from brilliant, and only a cat could have distinguished the oldest orange-woman from the prettiest grisette in Cordova.

One evening, when it was too dark to see anything, I was leaning against the parapet of the quay, smoking, when a woman ascended the steps leading to the river and seated herself by my side. She had in her hair a large bouquet of jasmine, the flowers of which exhale an intoxicating odour at night. She was simply, perhaps poorly clad, all in black, like most grisettes in the evening. Women of fashion wear black only in the morning; in the evening they dress *à la Francesca*. When she reached my side, my bather allowed the mantilla which covered her head to fall over her shoulders, and I saw, "by the dim light that falleth from the stars," that she was young, small, well built, and that she had very large eyes. I threw my cigar away at once. She appreciated that distinctively French attention, and made haste to say that she was very fond of the smell of tobacco; in fact, that she sometimes smoked herself, when she could obtain a very mild *papelito*. Luckily, I happened to have some of that description in my case, and I lost no time in offering them to her. She deigned to take one and lighted it at a piece of burning string which a child brought us in consideration of a small coin. Mingling our smoke, we talked so long, the fair bather and myself, that we were finally left almost alone on the quay. I thought that I might safely venture to invite her to take an ice at the *neveria*.* After hesitating modestly, she accepted; but before concluding to do so, she wished to know what time it was. I caused my repeater to strike, and that striking seemed to surprise her greatly.

"What wonderful things you foreigners invent! From what country are you, señor? An Englishman, no doubt?"†

"A Frenchman, and your humble servant. And you, señorita, or señora, are of Cordova, I presume?"

"No."

"You are an Andalusian, at all events. It seems to me that I can tell that by your soft speech."

"If you observe everybody's speech so closely, you should be able to guess what I am."

"I believe that you are from the land of Jesus, within two steps of paradise."

* A café provided with an ice-house, or rather with a store of snow. There is hardly a village in Spain which has not its *neveria*.

† In Spain every traveller who does not carry about with him specimens of calico or silk is taken for an Englishman, *Inglesito*. It is the same in the East; at Chalcia I had the honour of being announced as a *Μιλορδος Φραντζεσος* (French Milord).

(I had learned this metaphor, which designates Andalusia, from my friend Francisco Sevilla, a well-known picador.)

"Bah! paradise—the people about here say that it wasn't made for us."

"In that case you must be a Moor, or—"

I checked myself, not daring to say "Jewess."

"Nonsense! you see well enough that I am a gypsy; would you like me to tell your *baji*?* Have you ever heard of La Carmencita? I am she."

I was such a ne'er-do-well in those days—fifteen years ago—that I did not recoil in horror when I found myself seated beside a sorceress.

"Pshaw!" I said to myself. "Last week I supped with a highway robber, to-day I will pat ices with a handmaid of the devil. When one is travelling, one must see everything."

I had still another motive for cultivating her acquaintance. When I left school, I confess to my shame, I had wasted some time studying the occult sciences, and several times indeed I had been tempted to conjure up the spirits of darkness. Long since cured of my fondness for such investigations, I still retained, nevertheless, a certain amount of curiosity concerning all kinds of superstition, and I rejoiced at the prospect of learning how far the art of magic had been carried among the gypsies.

While talking together we had entered the *neveria* and had taken our seats at a small table lighted by a candle confined in a glass globe. I had abundant opportunity to examine

* Fortune.

my *gitana*, while divers respectable folk who were eating ices there lost themselves in amazement at seeing me in such goodly company.

I seriously doubt whether Señorita Carmen was of the pure breed; at all events, she was infinitely prettier than any of the women of her nation whom I had ever met. No woman is beautiful, say the Spaniards, unless she combines thirty *so*'s; or, if you prefer, unless she may be described by ten adjectives, each of which is applicable to three parts of her person. For instance, she must have three black things: eyes, lashes, and eyebrows, etc. (See Brantôme for the rest.) My gypsy could make no pretension to so many perfections. Her skin, albeit perfectly smooth, closely resembled the hue of copper. Her eyes were oblique, but of a beautiful shape; her lips a little heavy but well formed, and disclosed two rows of teeth whiter than almonds without their skins. Her hair, which was possibly a bit coarse, was black with a blue reflection, like a crow's wing, and long and glossy. To avoid fatiguing you with a too verbose description, I will say that for each defect she had some good point, which stood out the more boldly perhaps by the very contrast. It was a strange, wild type of beauty, a face which took one by surprise at first, but which one could not forget. Her eyes, especially, had an expression at once voluptuous and fierce, which I have never seen since in any mortal eye. "A gypsy's eye is a wolf's eye" is a Spanish saying which denotes keen observation. If you have not the time to go to the Jardin des Plantes to study the glance of a wolf, observe your cat when it is watching a sparrow.

Of course it would have been absurd to have my fortune

told in a café. So I requested the pretty sorceress to allow me to accompany her to her home. She readily consented, but she desired once more to know how the time was passing and asked me to make my watch strike again.

"Is it real gold?" she inquired, scrutinising it with extraordinary attention.

When we left the café, it was quite dark; most of the shops were closed, and the streets almost deserted. We crossed the Guadalquivir by the bridge, and at the very extremity of the suburb, we stopped in front of a house which bore no resemblance to a palace. A child admitted us. The gypsy said some words to him in a language entirely unknown to me, which I afterwards found was the *rommani* or *chipe calli*, the language of the *gitanos*. The child at once disappeared, leaving us in a room of considerable size, furnished with a small table, two stools, and a chest. I must not forget to mention a jar of water, a pile of oranges, and a bunch of onions.

As soon as we were alone, the gypsy took from her chest a pack of cards which seemed to have seen much service, a magnet, a dried chameleon, and a number of other articles essential to her art. Then she bade me make a cross in my left hand with a coin, and the magic ceremonies began. It is unnecessary to repeat her predictions; and, as for her method of operation, it was evident that she was not a sorceress by halves.

Unfortunately we were soon disturbed. The door was suddenly thrown open with violence, and a man wrapped to the eyes in a brown cloak entered the room, addressing the gypsy in a far from amiable fashion. I did not understand what he said, but his tone indicated that he was in a very bad temper. At sight of him the *gitana* exhibited neither surprise nor anger, but she ran to meet him, and, with extraordinary volubility, said several sentences in the mysterious tongue which she had already used in my presence. The word *payllo*, repeated several times, was the only word that I understood. I knew that the gypsies designated thus every man of another race than their own. Assuming that I was the subject of discussion, I looked forward to a delicate explanation; I already had my hand on one of the stools and was deliberating as to the precise moment when it would be well for me to hurl it at the intruder's head. But he roughly pushed the gypsy aside and strode toward me; then recoiled a step, exclaiming:

"What! is it you, señor?"

I looked closely at him and recognised my friend Don José. At that moment I was inclined to regret that I had not let him be hanged.

"Ah! is it you, my fine fellow?" I cried, laughing as heartily as I could manage to do. "You interrupted the señorita just as she was telling me some very interesting things."

"Always the same! This must come to an end," he said between his teeth, glaring savagely at the girl.

She meanwhile continued to talk to him in her own language. She became excited by degrees. Her eye became bloodshot and terrible to look at, her features contracted, and she stamped upon the floor. It seemed to me that she was earnestly urging him to do something which he evidently hesitated to do. What that something was, I fancied that

I understood only too well, when I saw her draw her little hand swiftly back and forth under her chin. I was tempted to believe that it was a matter of cutting a throat, and I had some suspicion that the throat in question was my own.

To all this torrent of eloquence Don José replied only by two or three words uttered in a sharp tone. Thereupon the gypsy bestowed on him a glance of supreme contempt; then seated herself Turkish fashion in a corner of the room, selected an orange, peeled it, and began to eat it.

Don José seized my arm, opened the door, and led me into the street. We walked about two hundred yards in absolute silence. Then he said, extending his hand:

"Go straight ahead and you will come to the bridge."

With that he turned his back on me and walked rapidly away. I returned to my inn rather sheepishly and in a very bad temper. The worst feature of the affair was that when I undressed I found that my watch was missing.

Various considerations deterred me from going the next day to demand it back, or from applying to the corregidor to recover it for me. I completed my work on the manuscript at the Dominican convent and departed for Seville. After wandering about Andalusia for several months, I determined to return to Madrid, and it was necessary for me to pass through Cordova once more. I did not propose to make a long stay there, for I had taken a violent dislike to that fair city and the bathers in the Guadalquivir. However, a few errands to do and some friends to call upon would detain me three or four days at least in the ancient capital of the Mussulman princes.

When I appeared at the Dominican convent, one of the fathers, who had taken a lively interest in my investigations concerning the location of Munda, welcomed me with open arms.

"Blessed be the name of God!" he cried. "Welcome, my dear friend! We all believed you to be dead, and I who speak to you, I have recited many *paters* and *aves*, which I do not regret, for the welfare of your soul. So you were not murdered?—for robbed we know that you were."

"How so?" I asked, not a little astonished.

"Why, yes—you know, that beautiful repeating watch that you used to make strike in the library when we told you that it was time to go to the choir. Well! it has been recovered; it will be restored to you."

"That is to say," I interrupted, somewhat disconcerted, "I lost it—"

"The villain is behind the bars, and as he was known to be a man who would fire a gun at a Christian to obtain a penny, we were terribly afraid that he had killed you. I will go to the corregidor's with you, and we will obtain your fine watch. And then, do not let me hear you whisper that justice does not know its business in Spain!"

"I confess," said I, "that I would rather lose my watch than give testimony in court which might send a poor devil to the gallows, especially because—because—"

"Oh! do not be alarmed on that score; he is well recommended, and he cannot be hanged twice. When I say hanged, I am wrong. He is a hidalgo, is your robber; so that he will be garroted* day after to-morrow, without fail. So, you see, one theft more or less will have no effect on his fate. Would to God that he had done nothing but steal! but he has committed several murders, each more shocking than the last."

"What is his name?"

"He is known throughout the province by the name of José Navarro, but he has another Basque name, which neither you nor I could ever pronounce. But he is a man worth looking at, and you, interested as you are in seeing all the curiosities of the province, should not neglect the opportunity to learn how villains leave this world in Spain. It will be in the chapel, and Father Martinez will take you thither."

My Dominican insisted so earnestly that I should view the preparations for the "pretty little hanging" that I could not refuse. I went to see the prisoner, having first supplied myself with a bunch of cigars, which, I hoped, would induce him to pardon my indiscretion.

I was ushered into the presence of Don José while he was eating. He nodded coldly to me, and thanked me courteously for the present I brought him. Having counted the cigars in the bunch which I placed in his hands, he took out a certain number and returned the rest to me, remarking that he should not need any more.

I asked him if I could make his lot any easier by the expenditure of a little money or by the influence of my friends. At

* In 1830 the nobility alone enjoyed that privilege. To-day (1847) under the constitutional *régime*, the plebeians have obtained the privilege of the *garrote*.

first he shrugged his shoulders and smiled sadly; but in a moment, on further reflection, he requested me to have a mass said for the salvation of his soul.

"Would you," he added timidly,—"would you be willing to have one said also for a person who injured you?"

"Certainly, my dear fellow," I said; "but there is no one in this part of the country who has injured me, so far as I know."

He took my hand and pressed it, with a solemn expression. After a moment's silence, he continued:

"May I venture to ask another favour at your hands? When you return to your own country, perhaps you will pass through Navarre; at all events, you will go by way of Vittoria, which is not very far away."

"Yes," I said, "I certainly shall go by way of Vittoria, but it is not impossible that I may turn aside to go to Pampelune, and, to oblige you, I think that I would willingly make that détour."

"Very well! if you go to Pampelune, you will see more than one thing that will interest you. It is a fine city. I will give you this locket (he showed me a little silver locket which he wore about his neck); you will wrap it in paper"—he paused a moment to control his emotion—"and deliver it, or have it delivered, to a good woman whose address I will give you. You will tell her that I am dead, but that you do not know how I died."

I promised to perform his commission. I saw him again the next day, and passed a large part of the day with him. It was from his own lips that I learned the melancholy adventures which follow.

III

"I was born," he said, "at Elizondo, in the valley of Baztan. My name is Don José Lizzarrabengoa, and you are familiar enough with Spain, señor, to know at once from my name that I am a Basque and a Christian of the ancient type. I use the title *Don* because I am entitled to it; and if I were at Elizondo, I would show you my genealogy on a sheet of parchment. My family wished me to be a churchman, and they forced me to study, but I profited little by it. I was too fond of playing tennis—that was my ruin. When we Navarrese play tennis, we forget everything. One day, when I had won, a young man from Alava picked a quarrel with me; we took our *maquilas*,* and again I had the advantage; but that incident compelled me to leave the country. I fell in with some dragoons, and I enlisted in the cavalry regiment of Almanza. The men from our mountains learn the military profession quickly. I soon became a corporal, with the promise of being promoted to quartermaster, when, to my undoing, I was placed on duty at the tobacco factory in Seville. If you have ever been to

* Ironshod staves carried by the Basques.

Seville, you must have seen that great building, outside of the fortifications, close to the Guadalquivir. It seems to me that I can see the doorway and the guard-house beside it at this moment. When on duty Spanish troops either gamble or sleep; I, like an honest Navarrese, always tried to find something to do. I was making a chain of brass wire, to hold my primer. Suddenly my comrades said: 'There goes the bell; the girls will be going back to work.' You must know, señor, that there are four or five hundred girls employed in the factory. They roll the cigars in a large room which no man can enter without a permit from the Twenty-four,* because they are in the habit of making themselves comfortable, the young ones especially, when it is warm. At the hour when the women return to work, after their dinner, many young men assemble to see them pass, and they make remarks of all colours to them. There are very few of those damsels who will refuse a silk mantilla, and the experts in that fishery have only to stoop to pick up their fish. While the others stared, I remained on my bench, near the door. I was young then; I was always thinking of the old province, and I did not believe that there were any pretty girls without blue petticoats and long plaited tresses falling over their shoulders.† Moreover, the Andalusian girls frightened me; I was not accustomed as yet to their manners: always jesting, never a serious word. So I had my nose over my chain, when I heard some civilians say: 'Here comes the

* The magistrate at the head of the police and municipal administration.
† The ordinary costume of the peasant women of Navarre and the Basque provinces.

gitanella!' I raised my eyes and I saw her. It was a Friday, and I shall never forget it. I saw that Carmen whom you know, at whose house I met you several months ago.

"She wore a very short red skirt, which revealed white silk stockings with more than one hole, and tiny shoes of red morocco, tied with flame-coloured ribbons. She put her mantilla aside, to show her shoulders and a huge bunch of cassia, which protruded from her chemise. She had a cassia flower in the corner of her mouth, too, and as she walked she swung her hips like a filly in the stud at Cordova. In my province a woman in that costume would have compelled everybody to cross themselves. At Seville every one paid her some equivocal compliment on her appearance, and she had a reply for every one, casting sly glances here and there, with her hand on her hip, as impudent as the genuine gypsy that she was. At first sight she did not attract me, and I returned to my work; but she, according to the habit of women and cats, who do not come when you call them, but come when you refrain from calling them,—she halted in front of me and spoke to me.

" '*Compadre*,' she said in Andalusian fashion, 'will you give me your chain to hold the keys of my strong-box?'

" 'It is to hold my primer' [*épinglette*], I replied.

" 'Your *épinglette*!' she exclaimed, with a laugh. 'Ah! the señor makes lace, since he needs pins!' [*épingles*]

"Everybody present began to laugh, and I felt the blood rise to my cheeks, nor could I think of any answer to make.

" 'Well, my heart,' she continued, 'make me seven ells of black lace for a mantilla, pincushion [*épinglier*] of my soul!'

"And, taking the flower from her mouth she threw it at me with a jerk of her thumb, and struck me between the eyes. Señor, that produced on me the effect of a bullet. I did not know which way to turn, so I sat as still as a post. When she had gone into the factory, I saw the cassia blossom lying on the ground between my feet; I do not know what made me do it, but I picked it up, unseen by my comrades, and stowed it carefully away in my pocket—the first folly!

"Two or three hours later, I was still thinking of her, when a porter rushed into the guard-house, gasping for breath and with a horrified countenance. He told us that a woman had been murdered in the large room where the cigars were made, and that we must send the guard there. The quartermaster told me to take two men and investigate. I took my two men and I went upstairs. Imagine, señor, that on entering the room I found, first of all, three hundred women in their chemises, or practically that, all shouting and yelling and gesticulating, making such an infernal uproar that you could not have heard God's thunder. On one side a woman lay on the floor, covered with blood, with an X carved on her face by two blows of a knife. On the opposite side from the wounded woman, whom the best of her comrades were assisting, I saw Carmen in the grasp of five or six women.

" 'Confession! Confession! I am killed!' shrieked the wounded woman.

"Carmen said nothing; she clenched her teeth and rolled her eyes about like a chameleon.

" 'What is all this?' I demanded. I had great difficulty in learning what had taken place, for all the work-girls talked at once. It seemed that the wounded one had boasted of having money enough in her pocket to buy an ass at the fair at Triana.

" 'I say,' said Carmen, who had a tongue of her own, 'isn't a broomstick good enough for you?' The other, offended by the insult, perhaps because she was conscious that she was vulnerable on that point, replied that she was not a connoisseur in broomsticks, as she had not the honour to be a gypsy or a godchild of Satan, but that the Señorita Carmencita would soon make the acquaintance of her ass, when the corregidor took her out to ride, with two servants behind to keep the flies away. 'Well!' said Carmen. 'I'll make watering-troughs for flies on your cheek, and I'll paint a checker-board on it.' And with that, *vli, vlan!* she began to draw St. Andrew's crosses on the other's face with the knife with which she cut off the ends of the cigars.

"The case was clear enough; I took Carmen by the arm. 'You must come with me, my sister,' I said to her courteously. She darted a glance at me, as if she recognised me; but she said, with a resigned air:

" 'Let us go. Where's my mantilla?'

"She put it over her head in such wise as to show only one of her great eyes, and followed my two men, as mild as a sheep. When we reached the guard-house, the quartermaster said that it was a serious matter, and that she must be taken to prison. It fell to my lot again to escort her there. I placed her between two dragoons, and marched behind, as a corporal should do under such circumstances. We started for the town. At first the gypsy kept silent; but on Rue de Serpent—

you know that street; it well deserves its name because of the détours it makes—she began operations by letting her mantilla fall over her shoulders, in order to show me her bewitching face, and turning toward me as far as she could, she said:

" 'Where are you taking me, my officer?'

" 'To prison, my poor child,' I replied, as gently as possible, as a good soldier should speak to a prisoner, especially to a woman.

" 'Alas! what will become of me? Señor officer, take pity on me. You are so young, so good looking!' Then she added, in a lower tone: 'Let me escape, and I'll give you a piece of the *bar lachi*, which will make all women love you.'

"The *bar lachi*, señor, is the lodestone, with which the gypsies claim that all sorts of spells may be cast when one knows how to use it. Give a woman a pinch of ground lodestone in a glass of white wine, and she ceases to resist.—I replied with as much gravity as I could command:

" 'We are not here to talk nonsense; you must go to prison—that is the order and there is no way to avoid it.'

"We natives of the Basque country have an accent which makes it easy for the Spaniards to identify us; on the other hand, there is not one of them who can learn to say even *bai, jaona*.* So that Carmen had no difficulty in guessing that I came from the provinces. You must know, señor, that the gypsies, being of no country, are always travelling, and speak all languages, and that most of them are perfectly at home in Portugal, in France, in the Basque provinces, in Catalonia,

* Yes, sir.

everywhere; they even make themselves understood by the Moors and the English. Carmen knew Basque very well.

" '*Laguna ene bihotsarena*, comrade of my heart,' she said to me abruptly, 'are you from the provinces?'

"Our language, señor, is so beautiful, that, when we hear it in a foreign land, it makes us tremble.—I would like to have a confessor from the provinces," added the bandit in a lower tone.

He continued after a pause:

" 'I am from Elizondo,' I replied in Basque, deeply moved to hear my native tongue spoken.

" 'And I am from Etchalar,' said she. That is a place about four hours journey from us. 'I was brought to Seville by gypsies. I have been working in the factory to earn money enough to return to Navarre, to my poor mother, who has no one but me to support her, and a little *barratcea*[*] with twenty cider-apple trees! Ah! if I were at home, by the white mountain! They insulted me because I don't belong in this land of thieves and dealers in rotten oranges; and those hussies all leagued against me, because I told them that all their Seville *jacques*[†] with their knives wouldn't frighten one of our boys with his blue cap and his *maquila*. Comrade, my friend, won't you do anything for a countrywoman?'

"She lied, señor, she always lied. I doubt whether that girl ever said a true word in her life; but when she spoke, I believed her: it was too much for me. She murdered the

* Enclosure, garden.

† Bravoes, bullies.

Basque language, yet I believed that she was a Navarrese. Her eyes alone, to say nothing of her mouth and her colour, proclaimed her a gypsy. I was mad, I paid no heed to anything. I thought that if Spaniards had dared to speak slightingly to me of the provinces, I would have slashed their faces as she had slashed her comrade's. In short, I was like a drunken man; I began to say foolish things, I was on the verge of doing them.

" 'If I should push you and you should fall, my countryman,' she continued, in Basque, 'it would take more than these two Castilian recruits to hold me.'

"Faith, I forgot orders and everything, and said to her:

" 'Well, my dear, my countrywoman, try it, and may Our Lady of the Mountain be with you!'

"At that moment we were passing one of the narrow lanes of which there are so many in Seville. All of a sudden Carmen turned and struck me with her fist in the breast. I purposely fell backward. With one spring she leaped over me and began to run, showing us a fleet pair of legs! Basque legs are famous; hers were quite equal to them—as swift and as well moulded. I sprang up instantly; but I held my lance horizontally so as to block the street, so that my men were delayed for a moment when they attempted to pursue her. Then I began to run myself, and they at my heels. But overtake her! there was no danger of that, with our spurs, and sabres, and lances!* In less time than it takes to tell it, the prisoner had disappeared. Indeed, all the women in the quarter favoured her flight, laughed at us, and sent us in the wrong direction.

* All the Spanish cavalry are armed with lances.

After much marching and countermarching, we were obliged to return to the guard-house without a receipt from the governor of the prison.

"My men, to avoid being punished, said that Carmen had talked Basque with me; and to tell the truth, it did not seem any too natural that a blow with the fist of so diminutive a girl should upset a fellow of my build so easily. It all seemed decidedly suspicious, or rather it seemed only too clear. When I went off duty I was reduced to the ranks and sent to prison for a month. That was my first punishment since I had been in the service. Farewell to the uniform of a quartermaster, which I fancied that I had already won!

"My first days in prison passed dismally enough. When I enlisted I had imagined that I should at least become an officer. Longa and Mina, countrymen of mine, are captains-general; Chapalangarra, who, like Mina, is a negro and is a refugee in your country—Chapalangarra was a colonel, and I have played tennis twenty times with his brother, who was a poor devil like myself. Now I said to myself: 'All the time that you have served without punishment is time thrown away. Here you are blacklisted, and to regain the good graces of your superiors, you will have to work ten times harder than when you first enlisted! And why did you receive punishment? For a gypsy hussy, who made a fool of you, and who is doubtless stealing at this moment in some corner of the city.'—But I could not help thinking of her. Would you believe it, señor? I had always before my eyes her silk stockings, full of holes, which she had shown me from top to bottom when she ran away. I looked through the bars into the street, and among all the women who passed I did not see a single one who could be compared with that devil of a girl! And then, too, in spite of myself, I smelt of the cassia flower she had thrown at me, which, although it had withered, still retained its sweet odour. If there are such things as witches, that girl was one!

"One day the jailer came in and gave me an Alcala* loaf.

" 'Here,' said he, 'your cousin sends you this.'

"I took the loaf, greatly surprised, for I had no cousin in Seville. 'It may be a mistake,' I thought as I glanced at the loaf; but it was so appetising, it smelt so good, that, without disturbing myself as to whence it came or for whom it was intended, I determined to eat it. On attempting to cut it my knife came in contact with something hard. I investigated and found a small English file, which had been slipped into the dough before baking. There was also in the loaf a gold piece of two piasters. There was no more doubt in my mind; it was a gift from Carmen. To people of her race freedom is everything, and they would set fire to a city to save themselves from a day in prison. However, she was a shrewd minx, and with that loaf one could snap one's fingers at jailers. In an hour's time the stoutest bar could be sawed through with the little file; and with the two piastres I could exchange my uniform for a civilian's coat at the first old clo'-man's. You may imagine that a man who had many a time taken young eaglets from their nests on our cliffs would not have been

* Alcala de los Panaderos, a hamlet two leagues from Seville, where they make delicious small loaves. It is claimed that their excellence is due to the water of Alcala, and great quantities of them are taken to Seville daily.

at a loss to climb down into the street from a window less than thirty feet high. But I did not wish to escape. I still possessed my honour as a soldier, and to desert seemed to me a heinous crime. However, I was touched by that token of remembrance. When you are in prison you like to think that you have a friend outside who is interested in you. The gold piece disturbed me a little, and I would have liked to return it; but where was I to find my creditor? That did not seem to me a simple matter.

"After the ceremony of reduction to the ranks, I thought that I could not suffer any more; but I had still another humiliation to undergo: when, on my release from prison, I was restored to duty and made to take my turn at sentry-go like any private. You cannot conceive what a man of spirit feels at such a time. I believe that I would as lief have been shot. Then, at all events, you walk alone, in front of the platoon; you feel that you are somebody; people look at you.

"I was stationed at the colonel's door. He was a wealthy young man, a good fellow who liked to enjoy himself. All the young officers were at his house, and many civilians—women, too, actresses, so it was said. For my own part, it seemed to me as if the whole city had arranged to meet at his door, in order to stare at me. Finally, the colonel's carriage drives up, with his valet on the box. Whom do I see alight from it?—the *gitanella*! She was arrayed like a shrine this time, bedizened and bedecked, all gold and ribbons. A spangled dress, blue slippers, also with spangles, and flowers and lace everywhere. She had a tambourine in her hand. There were two other gypsy women with her, one young and one old. There always is an old woman to go about with them. Then there was an old man, also a gypsy, with a guitar, to play for them to dance. You know that it is the fashion to hire gypsies to go about to parties, to dance the *romalis*—that is their national dance—and oftentimes for something else.

"Carmen recognised me and we exchanged a glance. I do not know why, but at that moment I would have liked to be a hundred feet underground.

" '*Agur laguna*,'* she said; 'you seem to be mounting guard, like a raw recruit, my officer!'

"And before I had thought of a word to say in reply, she was inside the house.

"The whole company was in the *patio*, and in spite of the crowd, I could see through the gate almost everything that took place.† I heard the castanets, the tambourine, the laughter and applause; sometimes I could see her head when she leaped into the air with her tambourine. And then I heard some of the officers say to her many things that brought the blood to my cheeks. I did not know what she replied. It was that day, I believe, that I began to love her in good earnest; for I was tempted three or four times to go into the *patio* and run my sabre into the bellies of those popinjays who were making love to her. My torture lasted a good hour; then the gypsies

* Good-day, comrade.

† Most of the houses in Seville have an interior courtyard surrounded by porticos. The inhabitants live there in summer. The courtyard is covered with canvas, which is kept wet during the day and removed at night. The gate into the street is almost always open, and the passage leading into the courtyard is closed by an iron gate of elaborate workmanship.

came out and the carriage took them away. Carmen, as she passed, glanced at me again with the eyes that you know, and said, very low:

" 'My countryman, when one likes nice fried things, one goes to Lillas Pastia's at Triana for them.'

"Nimble as a kid, she jumped into the carriage, the coachman whipped his mules, and the whole merry band drove away I know not where.

"You will readily guess that when I was relieved from duty I went to Triana; but I was shaved first, and brushed my clothes as for a dress parade. She was at Lillas Pastia's, an old gypsy, black as a Moor, who kept an eating-house, to which many civilians came to eat fried fish—especially, I rather think, since Carmen had taken up her quarters there.

" 'Lillas,' she said, as soon as she saw me, 'I shall do nothing more to-day. It will be light to-morrow.* Come, my countryman, let's go for a walk.'

"She put her mantilla over her face, and behold, we were in the street, I with no idea where we were going.

" 'Señorita,' I said, 'I believe that I have to thank you for a present which you sent me when I was in prison. I ate the bread; I shall use the file to sharpen my lance, and I shall keep it in memory of you; but here is the money.'

" 'My word! he has kept the money!' she exclaimed, laughing heartily. 'However, it's all the better, for I am not in funds. But what does it matter? the dog that keeps going always finds a bone.† Come on, we will eat it all up. You shall treat me.'

* *Mañana sera otro dia.*—A Spanish proverb.

† A gypsy proverb.

"We were walking in the direction of Seville. As we entered Rue de Serpent, she bought a dozen oranges and bade me put them in my handkerchief. A little farther on she bought bread and sausages, and a bottle of Manzanilla; and finally she entered a confectioner's shop. There she tossed on the counter the gold piece I had given back to her with another that she had in her pocket and some small silver; then she asked me for all that I had. I had only a *piecette* and a few *cuartos*, which I gave her, sorely vexed because I had no more. I thought that she intended to carry off the whole shop. She selected all the best and most expensive sweetmeats: *yemas*,* *turon*,† preserved fruits, so long as the money held out. All those things too I must needs carry in paper bags. Perhaps you know Rue de Candilejo, where there's a head of King Don Pedro the Justiciary?‡ That head should have suggested

---

* Sugared yolks of eggs.

† A kind of nougat.

‡ King Don Pedro, whom we call the *Cruel*, but whom Isabella the Catholic always called the *Justiciary*, loved to walk the streets of Seville at night in search of adventures, like the Caliph Haroun-al-Raschid. On a certain night he had a quarrel in an out-of-the-way street with a man who was giving a serenade. They fought and the king slew the love-lorn knight. Hearing the clash of swords, an old woman put her head out of a window and lighted up the scene with a small lamp (*candilejo*) which she held in her hand. You must know that King Don Pedro, who was very active and powerful, had one physical peculiarity: his knees cracked loudly when he walked. The old woman had no difficulty in recognizing him by means of that cracking. The next day the Twenty-four who was on duty came to the king to make his report. "Sire, there was a duel last night on such a street. One of the combatants was killed." "Have you discovered the murderer?" "Yes, sire." "Why is he not punished before now?" "I await your orders, sire." "Carry out the law." Now the king had recently issued a decree providing that every duellist should be beheaded, and that his head should be

some salutary reflections to my mind. We stopped in front of an old house on that street. She entered the passage and knocked at a door on the ground floor. A gypsy woman, a veritable handmaid of Satan, opened the door. Carmen said a few words to her in *rommani*. The old woman grumbled at first, and Carmen, to pacify her, gave her two oranges and a handful of bonbons, and allowed her to taste the wine. Then she put her cloak over her shoulders and escorted her to the door, which she secured behind her with an iron bar. As soon as we were alone, she began to dance and laugh like a mad woman, saying:

" 'You are my *rom*, and I am your *romi*!'*

"I stood in the middle of the room, laden with all her purchases, not knowing where to put them. She threw them all on the floor and jumped on my neck, saying:

" 'I pay my debts, I pay my debts! That is the law of the *cales*.'†

---

exposed on the battle-field. The Twenty-four extricated himself from the dilemma like a man of wit. He caused the head of a statute of the king to be sawed off, and exposed it in a recess in the middle of the street where the murder had taken place. The king and all the good people of Seville thought it an excellent joke. The street took its name from the lamp of the old woman, who was the sole witness of the adventure. Such is the popular tradition. Zuniga tells the story a little differently. (See *Anales de Sevilla*, vol. ii., p. 136.) However, there is still a Rue de Candilejo in Seville, and in that street a stone bust said to be a portrait of Don Pedro. Unfortunately the bust is a modern affair. The old one was sadly defaced in the seventeenth century, and the municipal government caused it to be replaced by the one we see to-day.

* *Rom*, husband; *romi*, wife.

† *Calo*: feminine *calli*; plural *cales*. Literally *black*—the name by which the gypsies call themselves in their own tongue.

"Ah! that day, señor! that day! When I think of it, I forget to-morrow!"

The bandit was silent for a moment; then, having relighted his cigar, he continued:

"We passed the whole day together, eating, drinking, and the rest. When she had eaten her fill of bonbons, like a child of six, she stuffed handfuls of them into the old woman's water-jar.—'That's to make sherbet for her,' she said. She crushed *yemas* by throwing them against the wall. "That's to induce the flies to let us alone,' she said. There is no conceivable trick and no folly that she did not commit. I told her that I would like to see her dance; but where was she to obtain castanets? She instantly took the old woman's only plate, broke it in pieces, and in a moment she was dancing the *romalis*, clapping the pieces of crockery in as perfect time as if they had been castanets of ebony or ivory. One was never bored with that girl, I assure you.

"Night came on and I heard the drums beating the retreat.

" 'I must go to quarters for the roll-call,' I said.

" 'To quarters?' she repeated, contemptuously. 'Are you a negro, pray, that you allow yourself to be led by a stick? You are a regular canary, in dress and in temper!* Go! you are a chicken-hearted fellow!'

"I remained, with my mind made up beforehand to the guard-room. The next morning, she was the first to mention parting.

" 'Look you, Joseito,' she said, 'have I paid you? According

* The Spanish dragoons wear a yellow uniform.

to our law, I owed you nothing, as you are a *payllo*; but, you are a comely youth, and you took my fancy. We are quits. Good-day.'

"I asked her when I should see her again.

" 'When you are less stupid,' she replied with a laugh. Then, in a more serious tone: 'Do you know, my son, that I believe that I love you a little bit? But it can't last. Dog and wolf don't live happily together for long. Perhaps, if you should swear allegiance to Egypt, I should like to be your *romi*. But this is foolish talk; it can never be. Believe me, my boy, you have come off cheap. You have met the devil, yes, the devil; he isn't always black, and he didn't wring your neck. I am dressed in wool, but I am no sheep.* Go and put a wax candle in front of your *majari*.† She has well earned it. Well, good-bye once more. Think no more of Carmencita, or she might be the cause of your marrying a widow with wooden legs.'‡

"As she spoke she removed the bar that secured the door, and once in the street, she wrapped herself in her mantilla and turned her back on me.

"She spoke truly. I should have been wise to think no more of her; but after that day on Rue de Candilejo, I could think of nothing else. I walked about all day long, hoping to meet her. I asked the old woman and the eating-house keeper for news of her. Both replied that she had gone to Laloro,§

* A gypsy proverb.
† Saint—the Blessed Virgin.
‡ The gallows, supposed to be the widow of the last man hanged.
§ The red (land).

which was their way of designating Portugal. Probably they said that in accordance with Carmen's instructions, but I very soon found out that they lied. Several weeks after my day on Rue de Candilejo, I was on duty at one of the gates of the city. A short distance from the gate there was a breach in the wall; men were at work repairing it during the day, and at night a sentinel was posted there to prevent smuggling. During the day I saw Lillas Pastia going to and fro around the guard-house, and talking with some of my comrades; all of them knew him, and they knew his fish and his fritters even better. He came to me and asked me if I had heard from Carmen.

" 'No,' said I.

" 'Well, you will, *compadre*.'

"He was not mistaken. At night I was stationed at the breach. As soon as the corporal had retired, I saw a woman coming towards me. My heart told me that it was Carmen. However, I shouted:

" 'Go back! You cannot pass!'

" 'Don't be disagreeable,' she said, showing me her face.

" 'What! is it you, Carmen?'

" 'Yes, my countryman. Let us talk a little and talk quick. Do you want to earn a *douro*. There are some men coming with bundles; let them alone.'

" 'No,' I replied. 'I must prevent them from passing; those are my orders.'

" 'Orders! orders! So you've forgotten the Rue de Candilejo?'

" 'Ah!' I exclaimed, completely overwhelmed by the bare

memory of that day. 'That would be well worth the penalty of forgetting orders; but I want no smugglers' money.'

" 'Well, if you don't want money, would you like to go again to old Dorothy's and dine?'

" 'No,' I said, half suffocated by the effort it cost me, 'I cannot.'

" 'Very good. If you are so stiff-backed, I know whom to apply to. I will go to your officer and offer to go to Dorothy's with him. He looks like a good fellow, and he will put some man on duty who will see no more than he ought to see. Farewell, Canary. I shall laugh with all my heart on the day when the orders are to hang you.'

"I was weak enough to call her back, and I promised to allow all gypsydom to pass, if necessary, provided that I obtained the only reward that I desired. She instantly swore to keep her word on the next day, and hastened away to notify her friends, who were close by. There were five of them,—Pastia was one—all well laden with English goods. Carmen kept watch. She was to give warning with her castanets the instant that she saw the patrol; but she did not need to do it. The smugglers did their work in an instant.

"The next day I went to Rue de Candilejo. Carmen kept me waiting, and when she came she was in a villainous temper.

" 'I don't like people who make you ask them so many times,' she said. 'You did me a very great service the first time, without knowing whether you would gain anything by it. Yesterday, you bargained with me. I don't know why I came, for I don't love you any more. Here, take this *douro* for your trouble.'

"I was within an ace of throwing the money at her head, and I was obliged to make a violent effort over myself to keep from striking her. After we had quarrelled for an hour, I left the house in a rage. I wandered about the city a long while, tramping hither and thither like a madman; at last I entered a church, and, seeking out the darkest corner, wept scalding tears. Suddenly I heard a voice:

" 'A dragoon's tears! I must make a love-philtre of them!'

"I raised my eyes; Carmen stood in front of me.

" 'Well, my countryman, are you still angry with me?' she said. 'It must be that I love you, in spite of what I know of you, for since you left me, I don't know what is the matter with me. See, I am the one now who asks you to come to Rue de Candilejo.'

"So we made our peace; but Carmen's moods were like the weather in our country. Among our mountains a storm is never so near as when the sun shines brightest. She promised to meet me again at Dorothy's, and she did not come. And Dorothy told me coolly that she had gone to Laloro on business of Egypt.

"As I knew already from experience what to think on that subject, I sought Carmen wherever I thought that she could possibly be, and I passed through Rue de Candilejo twenty times a day. One evening I was at Dorothy's having almost tamed her by treating her now and then to a glass of anisette, when Carmen came in, followed by a young officer, a lieutenant in our regiment.

" 'Off with you, quick,' she said to me in Basque.

"I sat as if stupefied, with rage in my heart.

" 'What are you doing here?' the lieutenant asked me. 'Decamp, leave this house!'

"I could not take a step; I was like a man who has lost the use of his limbs. The officer, seeing that I did not withdraw, and that I had not even removed my forage cap, lost his temper, seized me by the collar, and shook me roughly. I do not know what I said to him. He drew his sword, and I my sabre. The old woman grasped my arm, and the lieutenant struck me a blow on the forehead, the mark of which I still bear. I stepped back and knocked Dorothy down with a blow of my elbow; then, as the lieutenant followed me, I held the point of my sabre to his breast, and he spitted himself on it. Thereupon Carmen put out the lamp and told Dorothy in her language to fly. I myself rushed out into the street and started to run, I knew not whither. It seemed to me that some one was following me. When I came to my senses, I found that Carmen had not left me.

" 'You great idiot of a canary!' she exclaimed. 'You can't do anything but make a fool of yourself! I told you, you know, that I should bring you bad luck. Well! there's a cure for everything when one has for one's friend a Roman Fleming.* First of all, put this handkerchief on your head, and toss me that belt. Wait for me in this passage. I will return in two minutes.'

"She disappeared, and soon brought me a striped cloak,

* *Flamenco de Roma*—a slang term to designate a gypsy, *Roma* does not mean here the Eternal City, but the race of *Romi*, or married folk, a name which the gypsies assume. The first that were seen in Spain probably came from the Low Countries, whence the designation *Flemings*.

which she had obtained heaven knows where. She bade me take off my uniform and put on the cloak over my shirt. Thus attired, with the handkerchief with which she had bound up the wound on my head, I looked not unlike a peasant from Valencia, so many of whom came to Seville to sell their *chufas*[*] orgeat. Then she took me into a house much like Dorothy's, at the end of a narrow lane. She and another gypsy washed me and dressed my wound better than any surgeon could have done, and gave me something, I don't know what, to drink; finally, they laid me on a mattress, and I went to sleep.

"Probably those women had mingled with my drink one of those soporific drugs of which they know the secret, for I did not wake until very late the next day. I had a terrible headache and a little fever. It was some time before I remembered the terrible scene in which I had taken part the night before. After dressing my wound, Carmen and her friend, both squatting beside my mattress, exchanged a few words of *chipe calli*, which seemed to be a medical consultation. Then they united in assuring me that I should soon be cured, but that I must leave Seville at the earliest possible moment; for, if I should be caught, I would inevitably be shot.

" 'My boy,' said Carmen, 'you must do something. Now that the king gives you neither rice nor dried fish,[†] you must think about earning your living. You are too stupid to steal *à pastesas*;[‡] but you are strong and active; if you have any pluck,

---

* A bulbous root of which a very pleasant drink is made.

† The ordinary ration of the Spanish soldier.

‡ That is, with address, and without violence.

go to the coast and be a smuggler. Haven't I promised to be the cause of your being hung? That's better than being shot? However, if you go about it the right way you will live like a prince as long as the *miñons** and the coast-guards don't get their hands on your collar.'

"In this engaging way did that diabolical girl point out to me the new career for which she destined me, the only one, to tell the truth, which remained open to me, now that I had incurred the death penalty. Need I tell you, señor? she prevailed upon me without much difficulty. It seemed to me that I should become more closely united to her by that life of perils and of rebellion. Thenceforth I felt that I was sure of her love. I had often heard of a band of smugglers who infested Andalusia, mounted on good horses, blunderbuss in hand, and their mistresses *en croupe*. I imagined myself trotting over mountain and valley with the pretty gypsy behind me. When I spoke to her about it she laughed until she held her sides, and told me that there was nothing so fine as a night in camp, when every *rom* retires with his *romi* under the little tent formed of three hoops with canvas stretched over them.

" 'If I ever have you in the mountains,' I said to her, 'I shall be sure of you! There, there are no lieutenants to share with me.'

" 'Oh! you are jealous,' she replied. 'So much the worse for you! Are you really stupid enough for that? Don't you see that I love you, as I have never asked you for money?'

* A sort of unattached body of troops.

"When she talked like that I felt like strangling her.

"To cut it short, señor, Carmen procured a civilian's costume for me in which I left Seville without being recognised. I went to Jerez with a letter from Pastia to a dealer in anisette, whose house was a rendezvous for smugglers. There I was presented to those gentry, whose leader, one Dancaïre, took me into his troop. We started for Gaucin, where I found Carmen, who had agreed to meet me there. In our expeditions she served us as a spy, and a better spy there never was. She was returning from Gibraltar and she had already arranged with the master of a vessel to bring a cargo of English goods which we were to receive on the coast. We went to Estepona to wait for it, and concealed a portion in the mountains. Then, laden with the rest, we journeyed to Ronda. Carmen had preceded us thither, and it was she who let us know the opportune moment to enter the town. That first trip and several succeeding ones were fortunate. The smuggler's life pleased me better than that of a soldier. I made presents to Carmen; I had money and a mistress. I suffered little from remorse, for, as the gypsies say: 'The scab does not itch when one is enjoying one's self.' We were well received everywhere; my companions treated me well; and even showed me much consideration. The reason was that I had killed a man, and there were some among them who had not such an exploit on their consciences. But what appealed to me most strongly in my new life was that I saw Carmen often. She was more affectionate with me than ever; but before our comrades she would not admit that she was my mistress and she had even made me swear all sorts of oaths never to say anything about her. I was so weak before that creature that I obeyed all her whims. Moreover, it was the first time that she had exhibited herself to me with the reserve of a virtuous woman, and I was simple enough to believe that she had really corrected herself of her former manners.

"Our troop, which consisted of eight or ten men, seldom met except at critical moments; ordinarily we were scattered about by twos and threes, in different towns and villages. Each of us claimed to have a trade; one was a tinker, another a horse-dealer; I was a silk merchant, but I seldom showed my face in the large places because of my unfortunate affair at Seville.

"One day, or rather one night, our rendezvous was at the foot of Veger. Dancaïre and I arrived there before the rest. He seemed in very high spirits.

" 'We are going to have another comrade,' he said. 'Carmen has just played one of her best tricks. She has managed the escape of her *rom*, who was at the presidio at Tarifa.'

"I was already beginning to understand the gypsy tongue, which almost all my comrades spoke, and that word *rom* gave me a shock.

" 'What's that? her husband! is she married?' I asked the captain.

" 'Yes,' he replied, 'to Garcia the One-Eyed, a gypsy, as sharp as herself. The poor fellow was at the galleys. Carmen bamboozled the surgeon at the presidio so successfully that she has obtained her *rom*'s liberty. Ah! that girl is worth her weight in gold. For two years she has been trying to manage his escape. Every scheme failed until they took it into their heads to change surgeons. With the new one she seems to have found a way to come to an understanding very soon.'

"You can imagine the pleasure that that news afforded me. I soon saw Garcia the One-Eyed; he was surely the most loathsome monster that ever gypsydom reared; black of skin, and blacker of heart, he was the most unblushing villain that I have ever met in my life. Carmen came with him; and when she called him her *rom* in my presence you should have seen the eyes she made at me and her grimaces when Garcia turned his head. I was angry, and I did not speak to her that night. In the morning we had made up our bales and were already on the march, when we discovered that a dozen horsemen were at our heels. The braggart Andalusians, who talked of nothing but massacring everybody, made a most pitiful show. It was a general save himself who could. Dancaïre, Garcia, a handsome fellow from Ecija whom we called the Remendado, and Carmen, did not lose their heads. The rest had abandoned the mules, and had plunged into the ravines, where horses could not follow them. We could not keep our animals, and we hastily unpacked the best of our booty and loaded it on our shoulders, then tried to escape down the steep slopes of the cliffs. We threw our bundles before us and slid down on our heels after them as best we could. Meanwhile the enemy were peppering us; it was the first time that I had ever heard the whistle of bullets, and it didn't affect me very much. When one is under the eye of a woman, there is no merit in laughing at death. We escaped, all except the poor Remendado, who received a shot in the loins. I dropped my bundle and tried to carry him.

" 'Fool!' shouted Garcia. 'What have we to do with carrion? Finish him and don't lose the stockings!'

" 'Drop him!' Carmen called to me.

"Fatigue forced me to place him on the ground a moment, behind a rock. Garcia stepped up and discharged his blunderbuss at his head.

" 'It will be a clever man who will recognise him now,' he said, glancing at his face, which was torn to shreds by a dozen bullets.

"Such, señor, was the noble life I led. That night we found ourselves in a copse, utterly worn out and ruined by the loss of our mules. What does that infernal Garcia do but pull a pack of cards from his pocket and begin to play with Dancaïre by the light of a fire which they kindled. Meanwhile I had lain down and was gazing at the stars, thinking of the Remendado and saying to myself that I would rather be in his place. Carmen was sitting near me, and from time to time she played with the castanets and sang under her breath. Then, drawing nearer as if to speak to me, she kissed me, almost against my will two or three times.

" 'You are the devil!' I said to her.

" 'Yes,' she replied.

"After a few hours' rest she started for Gaucin, and the next day a young goatherd brought us food. We remained there the whole day, and at night went in the direction of Gaucin. We expected to hear from Carmen. No one appeared. At daybreak we saw a muleteer conducting a well-dressed woman with a parasol, and a small girl who seemed to be her servant. Garcia said:

“ ‘Here’s two mules and two women sent to us by Saint Nicholas; I should rather have four mules; but no matter, I’ll make the best of it.”

“He took his blunderbuss and crept down toward the path, keeping out of sight in the underbrush. We followed him, Dancaïre and I, at a short distance. When we were within arm’s length we showed ourselves and called to the muleteer to stop. The woman when she saw us, instead of being frightened—and our costumes were quite enough to frighten her—shouted with laughter.

“ ‘Ha! ha! the *lillipendi*, to take me for an *erani*!’*

“It was Carmen, but so perfectly disguised that I should not have recognised her if she had spoken a different tongue. She jumped down from her mule and talked for some time in a low tone with Dancaïre and Garcia, then said to me:

“ ‘We shall meet again, Canary, before you’re hung. I am going to Gibraltar on business of Egypt. You will hear of me soon.’

“We parted, after she had told us of a place where we could obtain shelter for a few days. That girl was the Providence of our party. We soon received some money which she sent us, and some information which was worth much more to us; it was to the effect that on such a day two English noblemen would leave Gibraltar for Grenoble by such a road. A word to the wise is sufficient. They had a store of good guineas. Garcia wanted to kill them, but Dancaïre and I objected. We took

* The idiots, to take me for a swell!

only their money and watches, in addition to their shirts, of which we were in sore need.

"Señor, a man becomes a rascal without thinking of it. A pretty girl steals your wits, you fight for her, an accident happens, you have to live in the mountains, and from a smuggler you become a robber before you know it. We considered that it was not healthy for us in the neighbourhood of Gibraltar, after the affair of the noblemen, and we buried ourselves in the Sierra de Ronda. You once mentioned José Maria to me; well, it was there that I made his acquaintance. He took his mistress on his expeditions. She was a pretty girl, clean and modest and well-mannered; never an indecent word, and such devotion. As a reward, he made her very unhappy. He was always running after women, he maltreated her, and sometimes he took it into his head, to pretend to be jealous. Once he struck her with a knife. Well, she loved him all the better for it. Women are made like that, especially the Andalusians. She was proud of the scar she had on her arm, and showed it as the most beautiful thing in the world. And then José Maria was the worst kind of a comrade, to boot. In an expedition that we made together, he managed matters so well that he had all the profit, we all the blows and trouble. But I resume my story. We heard nothing at all from Carmen.

" 'One of us must go to Gibraltar to find out something about her,' said Dancaïre. 'She should have arranged some affair for us. I would go, but I am too well known at Gibraltar.'

"The One-Eyed said:

" 'So am I too; everybody knows me there, and I've played

so many games on the lobsters![*] and as I have only one eye, I am hard to disguise.'

" 'Shall I go, then?' said I in my turn, overjoyed at the bare thought of seeing Carmen again. 'Tell me, what must I do?'

"The others said to me:

" 'Arrange it so as to go by sea or by San Roque, as you choose; and when you get to Gibraltar, ask at the harbour where a chocolate seller called Rollona lives; when you have found her, you can learn from her what's going on yonder.'

"It was agreed that we three should go together to the Sierra de Gaucin, where I was to leave my companions and go on to Gibraltar in the guise of a dealer in fruit. At Ronda, a man who was in our pay had procured me a passport; at Gaucin they gave me a donkey; I loaded him with oranges and melons, and started. When I reached Gibraltar, I found that Rollona was well known there, but that she was dead or had gone *to the ends of the earth*,[†] and her disappearance explained, in my opinion, the loss of our means of correspondence with Carmen. I put my donkey in a stable, and, taking my oranges, I walked about the city as if to sell them, but in reality to see if I could not meet some familiar face. There are quantities of riff-raff there from all the countries on earth, and it is like the Tower of Babel, for you cannot take ten steps on any street without hearing as many different languages. I saw many gypsies, but I hardly dared to trust them; I sounded

---

* A name which the common people in Spain give to the English, on account of the colour of their uniform.

† That is to say, to the galleys, or to all the devils.

them and they sounded me. We divined that we were villains; the important point was to know whether we belonged to the same band. After two days of fruitless going to and fro I had learned nothing concerning Rollona or Carmen, and was thinking of returning to my comrades after making a few purchases, when, as I passed through a street at sunset, I heard a woman's voice calling to me from a window: 'Orange-man!' I looked up and saw Carmen on a balcony, leaning on the rail with an officer in red, gold epaulets, curly hair—the whole outfit of a great noble. She too was dressed magnificently: a shawl over her shoulders, a gold comb, and her dress all silk; and the saucy minx—always the same!—was laughing so that she held her sides. The Englishman called to me in broken Spanish to come up, that the señora wanted some oranges; and Carmen said in Basque:

" 'Come up, and don't be surprised at anything.'

"In truth nothing was likely to surprise me on her part. I do not know whether I felt more joy or grief at seeing her again. There was a tall English servant with powdered hair, at the door, who ushered me into a gorgeous salon. Carmen instantly said to me in Basque:

" 'You don't know a word of Spanish; you don't know me.' Then, turning to the Englishman: 'I told you I recognised him at once as a Basque; you will hear what a strange tongue it is. What a stupid look he has, hasn't he? One would take him for a cat caught in a pantry.'

" 'And you,' I said to her in my language, 'have the look of a brazen-faced slut, and I am tempted to slash your face before your lover.'

" 'My lover!' she said. 'Did you really guess that all by yourself? And you are jealous of this simpleton? You are more of a fool than you were before our evenings in Rue de Candilejo. Don't you see, blockhead that you are, that I am doing the business of Egypt at this moment, and in the most brilliant fashion too? This house is mine, the lobster's guineas will be mine; I lead him by the end of the nose, and I will lead him to a place he will never come out of.'

" 'And I,' I said, 'if you go on doing the business of Egypt in this way, I will see to it that you won't do it again.'

" 'Ah! indeed! Are you my *rom*, to give me orders? The One-Eyed thinks it's all right, what business is it of yours? Oughtn't you to be content to be the only man who can say that he's my *minchorrò*?'*

" 'What does he say?' asked the Englishman.

" 'He says that he is thirsty and would like to drink a glass,' Carmen replied.

"And she threw herself on a couch, roaring with laughter at her translation.

"When that girl laughed, señor, it was impossible to talk sense. Everybody laughed with her. The tall Englishman began to laugh too, like the fool that he was, and ordered something to be brought for me to drink.

"While I was drinking:

" 'Do you see that ring he has on his finger?' she asked me. 'I will give it to you if you want.'

"I replied:

* My lover, or rather, my fancy.

" 'I would give a finger to have your lord on the mountains, each of us with a *maquila* in his hand.'

" '*Maquila*—what does that mean?' asked the Englishman.

" '*Maquila*,' said Carmen, still laughing, 'is an orange. Isn't that a curious word for orange? He says that he would like to give you some *maquila* to eat.'

" 'Yes?' said the Englishman. 'Well! bring some *maquila* to-morrow.'

"While we were talking, the servant entered and said that dinner was ready. Thereupon the Englishman rose, gave me a piastre, and offered Carmen his arm, as if she could not walk alone. Carmen, still laughing, said to me:

" 'I can't invite you to dinner, my boy; but to-morrow, as soon as you hear the drums beating for the parade, come here with some oranges. You will find a room better furnished than the one on Rue de Candilejo, and you will see whether I am still your Carmencita. And then we will talk about the business of Egypt.'

"I made no reply; and after I was in the street I heard the Englishman calling after me:

" 'Bring some *maquila* to-morrow!' and I heard Carmen's shouts of laughter.

"I went out, having no idea what I should do. I slept little, and in the morning I found myself so enraged with that traitress that I had resolved to leave Gibraltar without seeing her; but at the first beat of the drum all my courage deserted me; I took my bag of oranges and hurried to Carmen. Her blinds were partly open, and I saw her great black eye watching me. The powdered servant ushered me in at once; Carmen gave him an errand to do, and as soon as we were alone she burst out with one of her shouts of crocodile laughter and threw herself on my neck. I had never seen her so lovely. Arrayed like a Madonna, perfumed—silk-covered furniture, embroidered hangings—ah!—and I, dressed like the highwayman that I was!

" '*Minchorrò!*' said Carmen. 'I have a mind to smash everything here, to set fire to the house, and fly to the mountains!'

"And such caresses! and such laughter! and she danced, and she tore her falbalas; never did monkey go through more antics, more deviltry, more grimacing. When she had resumed her gravity:

" 'Listen,' she said, 'let us talk of Egypt. I want him to take me to Ronda, where I have a sister who's a nun (a fresh outburst of laughter here). We shall go by a place that I will let you know. Do you fall upon him; strip him clean! The best way would be to finish him; but,' she added, with a diabolical smile which she assumed at certain times, and no one had any desire to imitate that smile at such times,—'do you know what you must do? Let the One-Eyed appear first. Do you stay back a little; the lobster is brave and a good shot; he has good pistols. Do you understand?'

"She interrupted herself with a fresh burst of laughter that made me shudder.

" 'No,' I said, 'I hate Garcia, but he is my comrade. Some day, perhaps, I will rid you of him, but we will settle our accounts after the fashion of my country. I am a gypsy only by chance; and in certain things I shall always be a downright Navarrese, as the proverb says.'

"She retorted:

" 'You are a blockhead, a fool, a genuine *payllo*! You are like the dwarf who thinks he's tall when he can spit a long way. You don't love me—be off!'

"When she said 'be off!' I could not go. I promised to leave Gibraltar, to return to my comrades and wait for the Englishman; she, on her side, promised to be ill until it was time to leave Gibraltar for Ronda. I stayed at Gibraltar two more days. She had the audacity to come to see me at my inn, in disguise. I left the city; I, too, had my plan. I returned to our rendezvous, knowing the place and hour when the Englishman and Carmen were to pass. I found Dancaïre and Garcia waiting for me. We passed the night in a wood beside a fire of pine cones, which blazed finely. I proposed a game of cards to Garcia. He accepted. In the second game I told him he was cheating; he began to laugh. I threw the cards in his face. He tried to take his gun, but I put my foot on it and said to him: 'They say you can handle a knife like the best *jaque* in Malaga—will you try it with me?' Dancaïre tried to separate us. I had struck Garcia two or three times with my fist. Anger made him brave; he drew his knife and I mine. We both told Dancaïre to give us room and a fair field. He saw that there was no way of stopping us, and he walked away. Garcia was bent double, like a cat on the point of springing at a mouse. He held his hat in his left hand to parry, his knife forward. That is the Andalusian guard. I took my stand Navarrese fashion, straight in front of him, with the left arm raised, the left leg forward, and the knife along the right thigh. I felt stronger than a giant. He rushed on me like a flash; I turned on my left foot, and he found nothing in front of him; but I caught him in the throat, and my knife went in so far that my hand was under his chin. I twisted the blade so sharply that it broke. That was the end. The knife came out of the wound, forced by a stream of blood as big as your arm. He fell to the ground as stiff as a stake.

" 'What have you done?' Dancaïre asked me.

" 'Look, you,' said I; 'we couldn't live together. I love Carmen, and I wish to be her only lover. Besides, Garcia was a villain, and I remembered what he did to poor Remendado. There are only two of us left, but we are stout fellows. Tell me, do you want me for your friend, in life or death?'

"Dancaïre gave me his hand. He was a man of fifty.

" 'To the devil with love affairs!' he cried. 'If you had asked him for Carmen, he'd have sold her to you for a piastre. There's only two of us now; how shall we manage to-morrow?'

" 'Let me do it all alone,' I replied. 'I snap my fingers at the whole world now.'

"We buried Garcia and pitched our camp again two hundred yards away. The next day Carmen and her Englishman passed, with two muleteers and a servant.

"I said to Dancaïre:

" 'I will take care of the Englishman. Frighten the others—they are not armed.'

"The Englishman had pluck. If Carmen had not struck his arm, he would have killed me. To make my story short, I won Carmen back that day, and my first words to her were to tell her that she was a widow. When she learned how it had happened:

" 'You will always be a *lillipendi*!' she said. 'Garcia ought to have killed you. Your Navarrese guard is all folly, and he has put out the light of better men than you. It means that his time had come. Yours will come too.'

" 'And yours,' I retorted, 'unless you're a true *romi* to me.'

" 'All right,' said she, 'I've read more than once in coffee grounds that we were to go together. Bah! let what is planted come up!'

"And she rattled her castanets, as she always did when she wished to banish some unpleasant thought.

"We forget ourselves when we are talking about ourselves. All these details tire you, no doubt, but I shall soon be done. The life we were then leading lasted quite a long time. Dancaïre and I associated with ourselves several comrades who were more reliable than the former ones, and we devoted ourselves to smuggling, and sometimes, I must confess, we stopped people on the high-road, but only in the last extremity and when we could not do otherwise. However, we did not maltreat travellers, and we confined ourselves to taking their money. For several months I had no fault to find with Carmen; she continued to make herself useful in our operations, informing us of profitable strokes of business we could do. She stayed sometimes at Malaga, sometimes at Cordova, sometimes at Granada; but at a word from me, she would leave everything and join me at some isolated tavern, or even in our camp. Once only—it was at Malaga—she caused me some anxiety. I knew that she had cast her spell upon a very rich merchant, with whom she probably proposed to repeat the Gibraltar pleasantry. In spite of all that Dancaïre could say, I left him and went to Malaga in broad daylight; I sought Carmen and took her away at once. We had a sharp explanation.

" 'Do you know,' she said, 'that since you have been my *rom* for good and all I love you less than when you were my *minchorrò*? I don't choose to be tormented or, above all, to be ordered about! What I want is to be free and to do what I please. Look out that you don't drive me too far. If you tire me out I will find some good fellow who will serve you as you served the One-Eyed.'

"Dancaïre made peace between us; but we had said things to each other that remained on our minds and we were no longer the same as before. Soon after an accident happened to us. The troops surprised us, Dancaïre was killed, and two more of my comrades; two others were captured. I was seriously wounded and but for my good horse I should have fallen into the soldiers' hands. Worn out with fatigue, and with a bullet in my body, I hid in some woods with the only comrade I had left. I fainted when I dismounted, and I thought that I was going to die in the underbrush like a wounded rabbit. My comrade carried me to a cave that we knew, then he went in search of Carmen. She was at Granada, and she instantly came to me. For a fortnight she did not leave me a moment. She did not close an eye; she nursed me with a skill and attention which no woman ever showed for the man she loved best. As soon as I could stand she took me to Granada with the utmost secrecy. Gypsies find sure places of refuge everywhere, and I passed more than six weeks in a house within two doors of the corregidor who was looking for me. More than once as I looked out from behind a shutter I saw him pass. At last I was cured; but I had reflected deeply on my bed of pain and I proposed to change my mode of life. I spoke to Carmen of leaving Spain and of seeking an honest livelihood in the New World. She laughed at me.

" 'We were not made to plant cabbages,' said she; 'our destiny is to live at the expense of the *payllos*. Look, you, I have arranged an affair with Nathan Ben-Joseph of Gibraltar. He has some cotton stuffs that are only waiting for you, to pass the frontier. He knows that you are alive. He is counting on you. What would our Gibraltar correspondents say if you should go back on your word?'

"I allowed her to persuade me and I resumed my wretched trade.

"While I was in hiding in Granada there were some bull-fights which Carmen attended. When she returned she had much to say of a very skilful picador named Lucas. She knew the name of his horse and how much his embroidered jacket cost. I paid no attention to it. Juanito, my last remaining comrade, told me some days later that he had seen Carmen with Lucas in a shop on the Zacatin. That began to disturb me. I asked Carmen how and why she had made the picador's acquaintance.

" 'He's a fellow with whom one can do business,' she said. 'A river that makes a noise has either water or stones. He won twelve hundred reals in the bull-fights. One of two things must happen: either we must have that money, or else, as he's a good rider and a fellow of good pluck, we must take him into our band. Such a one and such a one are dead and you need some one in their places. Take him.'

" 'I don't want either his money or his person,' I said, 'and I forbid you to speak to him.'

" 'Beware!' said she. 'When any one defies me to do a thing it's soon done!'

"Luckily the picador left for Malaga, and I turned my attention to bringing in the Jew's bales of cotton. I had a great deal to do in that affair, and so did Carmen; and I forgot Lucas; perhaps she forgot him, too, for the moment at least. It was about that time, señor, that I met you, first near Montilla, then at Cordova. I will say nothing about our last interview. Perhaps you remember it better than I do. Carmen stole your watch; she wanted your money, too, and above all, that ring that I see on your finger, which, she said, was a magnificent ring, which it was most important for her to own. We had a violent quarrel, and I struck her. She turned pale and shed tears, and that produced a terrible effect on me. I asked her to forgive me, but she sulked a whole day, and, when I started to return to Montilla, she refused to kiss me. My heart was very heavy, when, three days later, she came to see me with a laughing face and gay as a lark. Everything was forgotten, and we were like lovers of two days' standing. At the moment of parting, she said to me:

" 'There's to be a fête at Cordova; I am going to it, and I shall find out what people are going away with money and let you know.'

"I let her go. When I was alone, I mused upon that fête and upon Carmen's change of humour. 'She must have had her revenge already,' I thought, 'as she was the first to make advances.' A peasant told me that there were bulls at Cordova. My blood began to boil, and like a madman, I started for the city and went to the public square. Lucas was pointed out to me, and on the bench next to the barrier, I recognised Carmen. A single glance at her was enough to satisfy me. Lucas, when the first bull appeared, played the gallant, as I had foreseen. He tore the cockade* from the bull and carried it to Carmen, who instantly put it in her hair. The bull took it upon himself to avenge me. Lucas was thrown down, with his horse across his chest and the bull on top of them both. I looked for Carmen; she was no longer in her seat. It was impossible for me to leave the place where I was, and I was compelled to wait until the end of the sports. Then I went to the house that you know, and I lay in wait there all the evening and part of the night. About two o'clock Carmen returned, and was rather surprised to see me.

" 'Come with me,' I said to her.

" 'All right!' said she. 'Let us go.'

"I went for my horse and took her behind me, and we rode all the rest of the night without exchanging a word. At daybreak we stopped at a lonely *venta*, near a little hermitage. There I said to Carmen:

" 'Listen; I will forget everything; I will never say a word to you about anything that has happened; but promise me

---

* *La divisa*, a bow of ribbon, the colour of which indicates the place from which the bull comes. This bow is fastened in the bull's hide by a hook, and it is the very climax of gallantry to tear it from the living animal and present it to a woman.

one thing—that you will go to America with me and remain quietly there.'

" 'No,' she said, sullenly, 'I don't want to go to America. I am very well off here.'

" 'That is because you are near Lucas; but understand this, if he recovers, he won't live to have old bones. But, after all, why should I be angry with him? I am tired of killing all your lovers; you are the one I will kill.'

"She looked earnestly at me with that savage look of hers, and said:

" 'I have always thought that you would kill me. The first time I saw you, I had just met a priest at the door of my house. And that night when we left Cordova, didn't you see anything? A hare crossed the road between your horse's feet. It is written.'

" 'Carmen, don't you love me any more?' I asked her.

"She made no reply. She was seated with her legs crossed, on a mat, and making figures on the ground with her finger.

" 'Let us change our mode of life, Carmen,' I said to her in suppliant tone. 'Let us go somewhere to live where we shall never be parted. You know, we have a hundred and twenty ounces buried under an oak, not far from here. Then, too, we have funds in the Jew Ben-Joseph's hands.'

"She smiled and said:

" 'Me first, then you. I know that it is bound to happen so.'

" 'Reflect,' I continued; 'I am at the end of my patience and my courage; make up your mind, or I shall make up mine.'

"I left her and walked in the direction of the hermitage. I found the hermit praying. I waited until his prayer was at an end; I would have liked to pray, but I could not. When he rose I went to him.

" 'Father,' I said, 'will you say a prayer for some one who is in great danger?'

" 'I pray for all who are afflicted,' he said.

" 'Can you say a mass for a soul which perhaps is soon to appear before its Creator?'

" 'Yes,' he replied, gazing fixedly at me.

"And, as there was something strange in my manner, he tried to make me talk.

" 'It seems to me that I have seen you before,' he said.

"I placed a piastre on his bench.

" 'When will you say the mass?' I asked.

" 'In half an hour. The son of the innkeeper yonder will come soon to serve it. Tell me, young man, have you not something on your conscience which torments you? Will you listen to the advice of a Christian?'

"I felt that I was on the point of weeping. I told him that I would come again, and I hurried away. I lay down on the grass until I heard the bell ring. Then I returned, but I remained outside the chapel. When the mass was said, I returned to the *venta*. I hoped that Carmen would have fled—she might have taken my horse and made her escape—but I found her there. She did not propose that any one should say that I had frightened her. During my absence she had ripped the hem of her dress, to take out the lead. Now she was standing by a table, watching the lead, which she had melted and had just thrown into a bowl filled with water. She was so engrossed by her magic that she did not notice my return at first. At one moment she would take up a piece of lead and turn it in every direction with a melancholy air; then she would sing one of those ballads of magic in which they invoke Maria Padilla, Don Pedro's mistress, who, they say, was the *Bari Crallisa*, or the great queen of the gypsies.*

" 'Carmen,' I said, 'will you come with me?'

"She rose, pushed her bowl away, and put her mantilla over her head, as if ready to start. My horse was brought, she mounted behind me, and we rode away.

" 'So, my Carmen,' I said, after we had ridden a little way, 'you will go with me, won't you?'

" 'I will go with you to death, yes, but I won't live with you any more.'

"We were in a deserted ravine; I stopped my horse.

" 'Is this the place?' she said.

"And with one spring she was on the ground. She took off her mantilla, dropped it at her feet, and stood perfectly still, with one hand on her hip, looking me in the eye.

" 'You mean to kill me, I can see that,' she said; 'it is written, but you will not make me yield.'

" 'Be reasonable, I beg,' I said to her. 'Listen to me. All of the past is forgotten. However, as you know, it was you who ruined me; it was for your sake that I became a robber and a

* Maria Padilla has been accused of having bewitched King Don Pedro. A popular tradition says that she presented to Queen Blanche de Bourbon a golden girdle, which seemed to the fascinated eyes of the king a living serpent. Hence the repugnance which he always displayed for the unfortunate princess.

murderer. Carmen! my Carmen! let me save you and myself with you.'

" 'José,' she replied, 'you ask something that is impossible. I no longer love you; you do still love me, and that is the reason you intend to kill me. I could easily tell you some lie; but I don't choose to take the trouble. All is over between us. As my *rom*, you have a right to kill your *romi*; but Carmen will always be free. *Calli* she was born, *calli* she will die.'

" 'Then you love Lucas?' I demanded.

" 'Yes, I did love him, as I loved you, for a moment—but less than I loved you, I think. Now, I love nobody, and I hate myself for having loved you.'

"I threw myself at her feet, I took her hands, I drenched them with my tears. I reminded her of all the blissful moments we had passed together. I offered to remain a brigand to please her. Everything, señor, everything; I offered her everything, if only she would love me again.

"She said to me:

" 'To love you again is impossible. I will not live with you.'

"Frenzy took possession of me. I drew my knife. I would have liked her to show some fear and to beg for mercy, but that woman was a demon.

" 'For the last time,' I cried, 'will you stay with me?'

" 'No! no! no!' she replied, stamping the ground with her foot.

"And she took from her finger a ring I had given her and threw it into the underbrush.

"I struck her twice. It was the One-Eyed's knife, which

I had taken, having broken my own. She fell at the second stroke, without a sound. I fancy that I still see her great black eye gazing at me; then it grew dim and closed. I remained utterly crushed beside that corpse for a long hour. Then I remembered that Carmen had often told me that she would like to be buried in a wood. I dug a grave with my knife and laid her in it. I hunted a long while for her ring and found it at last. I placed it in the grave with her, also a small crucifix. Perhaps I did wrong. Then I mounted my horse, galloped to Cordova, and gave myself up at the first guard-house. I said that I had killed Carmen, but I have refused to tell where her body is. The hermit was a holy man. He prayed for her! He said a mass for her soul. Poor child! The *Cales* are guilty, for bringing her up so."

IV

Spain is one of those countries where we find to-day in the greatest numbers those nomads who are scattered over all Europe, and are known by the names of *Bohemians*, *Gitanos*, *Gypsies*, *Zigeuner*, etc. Most of them live, or rather lead a wandering existence, in the provinces of the south and east, in Andalusia, Estremadura, and the kingdom of Murcia; there are many in Catalonia. These latter often cross the frontier into France. They are to be seen at all the fairs in the Midi. Ordinarily the men carry on the trades of horse-dealer, veterinary, and clipper of mules; they combine therewith the industry of mending kettles and copper implements, to say nothing of smuggling and other illicit traffic. The women tell fortunes, beg, and sell all sorts of drugs, innocent or not.

The physical characteristics of the gypsy are easier to distinguish than to describe, and when you have seen a single one, you can readily pick out a person of that race from a thousand others. Features and expression—these above all else separate them from the natives of the countries where they are found. Their complexion is very dark, always darker than that of the peoples among whom they live. Hence the name *Cale*—black—by which they often refer to themselves. Their eyes, which are perceptibly oblique, well-shaped, and very black, are shaded by long, thick lashes. One can compare their look to nothing save that of a wild beast. Audacity and timidity are depicted therein at once, and in that respect their eyes express accurately enough the character of the race—crafty, insolent, but *naturally afraid of blows*, like Panurge. As a general rule, the men are well-knit, slender, and active; I believe that I have never seen a single one overburdened with flesh. In Germany, the gypsy women are often very pretty; beauty is very rare among the *gitanas* of Spain. When they are very young, they may pass for rather attractive ugly women; but when they have once become mothers, they are repulsive. The uncleanliness of both sexes is beyond belief, and one who has never seen the hair of a gypsy matron would find it hard to form an idea of it, even by imagining it as like the coarsest, greasiest, dustiest horsehair. In some large cities of Andalusia, some of the girls who are a little more attractive than the rest take more care of their persons. They go about dancing for money—dances very like those which are forbidden at our (Parisian) public balls during the Carnival. M. Borrow, an English missionary, the author of two very interesting works on the gypsies of Spain, whom he had undertaken to convert at the expense of the Bible Society, asserts that there is no known instance of a *gitana* having a weakness for a man not of her race. It seems to me that there is much exaggeration in the eulogium which he bestows on their chastity. In the first place, the great majority of them are in the plight of Ovid's ugly woman: *Casta quam nemo rogavit*. As for the pretty ones, they are, like Spanish women, exacting in the choice of their lovers. A man must please them and deserve them. M. Borrow cites as a proof of their virtue an instance which does honour to his own virtue, and above all to his innocence. An immoral man of his acquaintance, he says, offered several ounces of gold to a pretty *gitana*, to no purpose. An Andalusian to whom I told this anecdote declared that that same immoral man would have had better luck if he had shown only two or three piastres, and that to offer ounces of gold to a gypsy was as poor a way to persuade her as to promise a million or two to a servant girl at an inn. However that may be, it is certain that the *gitanas* display a most extraordinary devotion to their husbands. There is no peril or privation which they will not defy, in order to assist them in their need. One of the names by which the gypsies call themselves—*romi* or *spouses*—seems to me to bear witness to the respect of the race for the marriage state. In general, we may say that their principal virtue is patriotism, if we may call by that name the fidelity which they observe in their relations with persons of the same origin as themselves, the zeal with which they help one another, and the inviolable secrecy which they maintain in respect to compromising affairs. Indeed, we may remark something similar in all associations that are shrouded in mystery and are outside of the law.

A few months ago, I visited a tribe of gypsies settled in the Vosges. In the cabin of an old woman, the patriarch of the tribe, there was a gypsy unknown to her family, suffering from a fatal disease. That man had left a hospital, where he was well cared for, to die among his compatriots. For thirteen weeks he had been in bed in the cabin of his hosts, and much better treated than the sons and sons-in-law who lived in the same house. He had a comfortable bed of straw and moss, with reasonably white sheets, whereas the rest of the family, to the number of eleven, slept on boards three feet long. So much for their hospitality. The same woman who was so humane to her guest said in his presence: "*Singo, singo, homte hi mulo.*" "Before long, before long, he must die." After all, the life of those people is so wretched that the certainty of death has no terrors for them.

A remarkable feature of the gypsy character is their indifference in the matter of religion. Not that they are atheists or skeptics. They have never made profession of atheism. Far from that, they adopt the religion of the country in which they live; but they change when they change countries. The superstitions which among ignorant peoples replace religious sentiments are equally foreign to them. Indeed, how could superstition exist among people who, in most cases, live on the credulity of others! I have observed, however, among Spanish gypsies, a strange horror at the thought of touching a dead body. There are few of them whom money could hire to carry a corpse to the cemetery.

I have said that most gypsy women dabble in fortune-telling. They are very skilful at it. But another thing that is a source of very great profit to them is the sale of charms and love-philtres. Not only do they keep frogs' feet to fix fickle hearts, or powdered lodestone to force the unfeeling to love;

but at need they make potent conjurations which compel the devil to lend them his aid. Last year a Spanish woman told me the following story: She was passing one day along Rue d'Alcala, sad and distraught, when a gypsy sitting on the sidewalk called after her: "Your lover has been false to you, fair lady."—It was the truth.—"Do you want me to bring him back?"—You will imagine how joyfully the offer was accepted, and what unbounded confidence was naturally inspired by a person who could thus divine at a glance the inmost secrets of the heart. As it would have been impossible to proceed to magic rites in the most frequented street in Madrid, they made an appointment for the morrow—"Nothing easier than to bring the unfaithful one back to your feet," said the *gitana*. "Have you a handkerchief, a scarf, or a mantilla that he has given you?"—The lady gave her a silk handkerchief.—"Now sew a piastre into a corner of it, with crimson silk; half a piastre into another; a *piecette* here; a two-real piece here. Then you must sew a gold piece in the centre; a doubloon would be best."—The doubloon and the rest were duly sewn into the handkerchief.—"Now, give it to me; I will take it to the Campo-Santo when the clock strikes twelve. Come with me, if you want to see some fine deviltry. I promise you that you will see the man you love to-morrow."—The gypsy started alone for the Campo-Santo, for the lady was too much afraid of the devils to accompany her. I leave you to guess whether the poor love-lorn creature saw her handkerchief or her faithless lover again.

Despite their poverty and the sort of aversion which they inspire, the gypsies enjoy a certain consideration none the less among unenlightened peoples, and they are very proud of it. They feel a haughty contempt for intelligence, and cordially despise the people who give them hospitality. "The Gentiles are such fools," said a gypsy of the Vosges to me one day, "that there's no merit in tricking them. The other day a peasant woman called to me on the street, and I went into her house. Her stove was smoking and she asked me for a spell, to make it burn. I told her to give me first of all a big piece of pork. Then I mumbled a few words in *rommani*. 'You are a fool,' I said, 'you were born a fool, a fool you will die.'—When I was at the door, I said to her in good German: 'The infallible way to keep your stove from smoking is not to make any fire in it.'—And I ran off at full speed."

The history of the gypsies is still a problem. To be sure, we know that the first bands of them, very small in numbers, showed themselves in the east of Europe early in the fifteenth century; but no one can say whence they came to Europe, or why; and, which is more extraordinary, we have no idea how they multiplied so prodigiously, in a short time, in several countries at a great distance from one another. The gypsies themselves have preserved no tradition concerning their origin, and, although most of them speak of Egypt as their original fatherland, it is because they have adopted a fable that was spread abroad concerning them many, many years ago.

Most Orientalists who have studied the gypsy language believe that they came originally from India. In fact, it seems that a great number of the roots of the *rommani* tongue and many of its grammatical forms are found in phrases derived from the Sanskrit. We can understand that, in their long wanderings, the gypsies may have adopted many foreign words. In all the dialects of the *rommani*, we find many Greek words. For example: *cocal*, bone, from *χόχχαλον* (Greek); *petalli*, horseshoe, from *πεταλον* (Greek); *cafi*, nail, from *χαρφι* (Greek), etc. To-day, the gypsies have almost as many different dialects as there are bands of their race living apart from one another. Everywhere they speak the language of the country in which they live more readily than their own, which they seldom use except as a means of speaking freely before strangers. If we compare the dialect of the gypsies of Germany with that of the Spaniards, who have had no communication with the former for centuries, we discover a very great number of words common to the two; but the original tongue has been noticeably modified everywhere, although in different degrees, by the contact with the more cultivated tongues, which these nomads have been constrained to employ. German on the one side, Spanish on the other, have so modified the substance of the *rommani* that it would be impossible for a gypsy of the Black Forest to converse with one of his Andalusian brethren, although they need only exchange a few sentences to realise that each of them is speaking a dialect derived from the same parent tongue. A few words in very frequent use are common, I believe, to all dialects; for instance, in all the vocabularies which I have had an opportunity to see, *pani* means water, *manro*, bread, *mas*, meat, and *lon*, salt.

The names of the numbers are almost the same everywhere. The German dialect seems to me much purer than the Spanish; for it has retained a number of the primitive grammatical forms, while the *gitanos* have adopted those of the Castilian tongue. A few words, however, are exceptions to this rule and attest the former community of the dialects. The preterit tenses in the German dialect are formed by adding *ium* to the imperative, which is always the root of the verb. The verbs in the Spanish *rommani* are all conjugated like Castilian verbs of the first conjugation. From the infinitive *jamar*, to eat, they regularly make *jamé*, I have eaten; from *lillar*, to take, *lillé*, I have taken. But some old gypsies say, on the other hand, *jayon*, *lillon*. I know no other verbs which have retained this ancient form.

While I am thus parading my slight acquaintance with the *rommani* tongue, I must note a few words of French argot, which our thieves have borrowed from the gypsies. The *Mystères de Paris* has taught good society that *chourin* means knife. The word is pure *rommani*; *tchouri* is one of the words common to all the dialects. M. Vidocq calls a horse *grès*—that is another *rommani* word—*gras*, *gre*, *graste*, *gris*. Add the word *romanichel*, which in Parisian slang means gypsies. It is a corruption of *rommane tchave*, gypsy youths. But an etymology of which I am proud is that of *frimousse*; expression, face—a word which all schoolboys use, or did use in my day. Observe first that Oudin, in his curious dictionary, wrote in 1640 *firlimouse*. Now, *firla*, *fila*, in *rommani* means face; *mui* has the same meaning, it exactly corresponds to the Latin *os*.

The combination *firlamui* was instantly understood by a gypsy purist, and I believe it to be in conformity with the genius of his language. This is quite enough to give the readers of *Carmen* a favourable idea of my studies in *rommani*. I will close with this proverb, which is quite apropos: *En retudi panda nasti abela macha*—"a fly cannot enter a closed mouth."

1845

OTHER TITLES IN **THE ART OF THE NOVELLA SERIES**

BARTLEBY THE SCRIVENER
HERMAN MELVILLE

THE LESSON OF THE MASTER
HENRY JAMES

MY LIFE
ANTON CHEKHOV

THE DEVIL
LEO TOLSTOY

THE TOUCHSTONE
EDITH WHARTON

THE HOUND OF THE BASKERVILLES
ARTHUR CONAN DOYLE

THE DEAD
JAMES JOYCE

FIRST LOVE
IVAN TURGENEV

A SIMPLE HEART
GUSTAVE FLAUBERT

THE MAN WHO WOULD BE KING
RUDYARD KIPLING

MICHAEL KOHLHAAS
HEINRICH VON KLEIST

THE BEACH OF FALESÁ
ROBERT LOUIS STEVENSON

THE HORLA
GUY DE MAUPASSANT

THE ETERNAL HUSBAND
FYODOR DOSTOEVSKY

THE MAN THAT CORRUPTED HADLEYBURG
MARK TWAIN

THE LIFTED VEIL
GEORGE ELIOT

THE GIRL WITH THE GOLDEN EYES
HONORÉ DE BALZAC

A SLEEP AND A FORGETTING
WILLIAM DEAN HOWELLS

BENITO CERENO
HERMAN MELVILLE

MATHILDA
MARY SHELLEY

STEMPENYU: A JEWISH ROMANCE
SHOLEM ALEICHEM

FREYA OF THE SEVEN ISLES
JOSEPH CONRAD

HOW THE TWO IVANS QUARRELLED
NIKOLAI GOGOL

MAY DAY
F. SCOTT FITZGERALD

RASSELAS, PRINCE ABYSSINIA
SAMUEL JOHNSON

THE DIALOGUE OF THE DOGS
MIGUEL DE CERVANTES

THE LEMOINE AFFAIR
MARCEL PROUST

THE COXON FUND
HENRY JAMES

THE DEATH OF IVAN ILYCH
LEO TOLSTOY

TALES OF BELKIN
ALEXANDER PUSHKIN

THE AWAKENING
KATE CHOPIN

ADOLPHE
BENJAMIN CONSTANT

THE COUNTRY OF THE POINTED FIRS
SARAH ORNE JEWETT

PARNASSUS ON WHEELS
CHRISTOPHER MORLEY

THE NICE OLD MAN AND THE PRETTY GIRL
ITALO SVEVO

LADY SUSAN
JANE AUSTEN

JACOB'S ROOM
VIRGINIA WOOLF

THE DUEL
GIACOMO CASANOVA

THE DUEL
ANTON CHEKHOV

THE DUEL
JOSEPH CONRAD

THE DUEL
HEINRICH VON KLEIST

THE DUEL
ALEXANDER KUPRIN

THE ALIENIST
MACHADO DE ASSIS

ALEXANDER'S BRIDGE
WILLA CATHER

FANFARLO
CHARLES BAUDELAIRE

THE DISTRACTED PREACHER
THOMAS HARDY

THE ENCHANTED WANDERER
NIKOLAI LESKOV

THE NARRATIVE OF ARTHUR GORDON PYM OF NANTUCKET
EDGAR ALLAN POE

CARMEN
PROSPER MÉRIMÉE

THE DIAMOND AS BIG AS THE RITZ
F. SCOTT FITZGERALD

THE HAUNTED BOOKSHOP
CHRISTOPHER MORLEY

THE POOR CLARE
ELIZABETH GASKELL

THIS IS A MELVILLE HOUSE ▣ HYBRIDBOOK

HybridBooks are a union of print and electronic media designed to provide a unique reading experience by offering additional curated material—Illuminations—which expand the world of the book through text and illustrations.

Scan the code or follow the link below to gain access to the Illuminations for *Carmen* by Prosper Mérimée, including:

- Mérimée's watercolor painting of Carmen and Don José
- A guide to the gypsy language *chipe calli*
- An excerpt from Miguel de Cervantes's little-known gypsy tale, *La gitanilla*
- Selections from Mérimée's letters about his travels in Spain
- Images of the tobacco factory where Carmen works, then the largest industrial building in the world
- And many more readings and illustrations

Download a QR code reader in your smartphone's app store, or visit mhpbooks.com/merimee196